UNCHIPPED: THE REVENANT

THE UNCHIPPED SERIES
THE MEETING: AN UNCHIPPED SHORT STORY
UNCHIPPED: KAARINA
UNCHIPPED: WILLIAM
UNCHIPPED: ENYD
UNCHIPPED: LUNA
UNCHIPPED: THE RESORT
CHIPPED: LAURA
CHIPPED: DENNIS
CHIPPED: MARGARET
CHIPPED: JOVAN
CHIPPED: THE REVENANT
DECHIPPED: KRISTIAN
DECHIPPED: MARIA
DECHIPPED: OWENA
DECHIPPED: IRIS
DECHIPPED: THE DOWNLOAD
RECHIPPED: CITY OF SERBIA
RECHIPPED: CITY OF ENGLAND
RECHIPPED: CITY OF CALIFORNIA
RECHIPPED: CITY OF FINLAND
RECHIPPED: THE BUTTON

COMING SOON!
THE MACHINA DEUS SERIES (2024)
SERF GIRL
FAMA GIRL
SLUM GIRL

UNCHIPPED:
THE REVENANT

TAYA DEVERE

DVM Press
Kaarningonkatu 11,
20740 Turku, Suomi-Finland

www.dvmpress.com
www.tayadevere.com

For information about special discounts available for bulk purchases, sales promotions, fund-raising and educational needs, contact sales@dvmpress.com

ISBN 978-952-7404-29-4 First Ebook Edition
ISBN 978-952-7404-30-0 First Print Edition

Cover Design © 2020 by Deranged Doctor Design - www.derangeddoctordesign.com

Cover Spine Design © 2022 by Chris DeVere

Editing by Christopher Scott Thompson, Lindsay Fara Kaplan, and Elle Fort

To those who have made mistakes in life.
To those wrestling with regret, shame, or sorrow.
You are not your past. You are what you do today.

CONTENTS

PINS AND NEEDLES

A short story in the world of the Unchipped series

The Mansion, City of California, 2089

"Can we read this tonight?"

Micky stares at the woman—or girl, really—her unnaturally calm, smooth face always a bit jarring to him. Like so many other things these days, Owena isn't what she seems on the outside. She's not a thirty-something-year-old woman, but a five-year-old kid. She's not a skilled assassin trying to murder those who fight against the Happiness-Program, but a lost child, trapped in a body that doesn't really belong to her.

"What's it about?" Micky asks, patting the spot on the floor next to him. The other girl, running her hand along a black-and-white bunny's fur, sits in the corner of the master suite. She looks up, intrigued.

"It's a story about a family," Owena says, staring into Micky's eyes.

"But which genre?"

Owena tics and tilts her head. The twitching makes Micky nervous. He peeks at the "cage-hat" made of wires and miscellaneous metal parts. The hat has been put aside on the room's gaming chair to wait for Owena's daily playtime outside the mansion. It's safe here. She doesn't need it inside the mansion.

Does she?

"Genre," Micky repeats, making little circles with his hands while trying to find the right words. "Like, is it a romance or a ghost story?"

Owena's head twitches and tilts to the other side.

"Happy or sad?" Micky asks, trying to ignore the girl's robotic gestures.

"The sticker on Mister Jenkins's shelf said 'Classics,'" Owena finally replies.

"Yeah, but . . . " Micky frowns, then smiles at Owena, waving her over. "Doesn't matter. You reading, or am I?"

With catlike movements, silent and smooth, Owena sits down next to Micky. It's so unfair for people to call her a robot. Or even a clone. Just like it's unfair for Micky to be slightly afraid of her at all times. She's a living, feeling being. If anything, Owena must have twice as much emotion as the rest of them, considering that she's two people inside of one.

As Owena starts reading the story, Micky grabs a blanket and several pillows from the bed. He places the blanket over their legs and spreads the pillows around them on the floor. It's not much of a fort, but it will do. Together they lean against the wall, Owena reading aloud and Micky investigating Sanna's serious face in the corner of the room. She's been quiet for a long time, seemingly lost in the presence of her pet bunny.

Wonder what it's like to be Doctor Solomon's kid, Micky thinks, knowing that it wouldn't be a good idea to ask. Ever since the rebel crew left the green city to hide here in the mansion, Sanna's refused to communicate with her mother up in the cloud.

Cloud, egg . . . clones and robots. Micky shakes his head and sighs silently. The gesture stops Owena from reading. Frowning, she looks up at him.

"Nothing," Micky says and shakes his head. "Just keep reading. I like the boy already. I think he's going to turn out to be a superhero or something."

"Classics are not children's books," Sanna says from the corner, still petting the bunny. "If it's a classic, it'll have real people in it, not superheroes."

"Um, excuse me," Micky says, pretending to be insulted. "Miles Morales? Anya Corazón? Are you really saying that Spider-Man and Spider-Woman aren't classics?"

"You're a classic," Sanna says, annoyance in her voice. She sticks her tongue out.

Micky laughs and chucks one of the fort pillows at Sanna, his aim several feet too short. "You're terrible at insults, *muchacha.*"

"You're an insult."

Before Micky can continue their fake argument, Owena taps on his shoulder fiercely. Grinning, Micky looks over and sees the finest frown of annoyance on her face. She lifts the book, raising her eyebrows just a quarter of an inch.

"Yes, yes," Micky says and lifts his hands in the air. "By all means. Let's keep reading the non-classic super-boy story."

"*You're a superboy,*" Sanna's voice echoes inside Micky's head.

Stop tapping me, you little shit, he replies silently, still grinning. *Owena's going to be mad. And nobody has a good time when Owena's mad.*

For the next half an hour, Micky and Sanna sit silently, listening to the story develop. The further Owena reads, the deeper into the fort Micky buries himself. His heart beats faster, and his fingers grasp the blanket tighter and tighter.

Okay, niña, he taps at Sanna. *I'm wrong, you're right. This is no superhero story. This is a fucked-up story.*

Sanna leaves the bunny on the floor and grabs a doll—the girl calls her Tina—from the bed and walks over to Owena. She offers the doll to her. "Can we do that needle poking thing instead? I don't like this story."

"Needle poking?" Micky asks, moving his puzzled gaze from one girl to another.

Owena looks up from the pages but doesn't take the doll from Sanna. "In the middle of the chapter?"

With a small pout on her lips, Sanna nods repeatedly. "I don't like it. It's stupid."

"Scary as hell," Micky breathes out, "but I wouldn't say it's *stupid*."

The annoyance on Sanna's face deepens. "Family members don't want to hurt each other like that. They protect each other, no matter what. Just like any people. They don't want to hurt someone they care about."

Micky considers this, then shakes his head at Sanna. "Sure, but Jack is obviously going a bit cuckoo. Okay, *very* cuckoo."

"Doesn't matter. You don't do that to beings you know."

"Beings?"

Quickly, Sanna turns her head to stare at the bunny in the corner. While looking at its long ears, she nods, like the two now agree on something. When she looks back at Micky, her chin raises an inch higher. With a stubborn look on her face, she says, "It's not believable that Jack would hurt Danny."

"Plausibility?" Micky asks, trying to keep a straight face. "That's your argument?"

The book slams shut. Owena jumps up from the floor and nods at the doll Sanna's holding. "I'll search the pantry for needles."

As Owena strolls out of the room, Micky struggles to find words. How is he supposed to keep up with these two and their tomfoolery?

"Don't worry, Micky." Sanna sits down in Owena's spot. Again, her eyes find her rabbit in the corner. The small critter stares back at her, its nose wiggling rapidly, its ears pointing toward the conversation. "You can finish the book later."

"That's okay. Getting dark anyway."

"What does that have to do with anything?"

Micky turns to look at the girl, wondering if she's serious or not. "That book doesn't make you scared at all? Not even the twins?"

Sanna hugs her legs against her chest and leans her cheek against her knees. "That's not . . . " she stops to think of the word, "*plausible* either. The twins are stupid too."

A brief laugh escapes Micky's lips. This girl. She's something else. A warm wave of compassion and joy washes through him.

"I think a lot of the story has to do with mental illness," he says, mirroring Sanna's pose. Downstairs, they hear the pantry door creaking open. Yeti or Maria will surely think Owena's about to pocket some more chocolate bars from the supposedly secret stash under the back shelf. "Maybe you're just too young to understand, *niña*."

Sanna narrows her eyes at him. "Or maybe you're too old." Her chin raises an inch more. "I'm telling you. It's stupid."

He runs his fingers over the book cover and considers Sanna's words. A family shouldn't turn against its own, that's true. Bill would never abandon Micky, neither would Maria. And he himself would do anything to protect them both. And not just them, but all the Unchipped friends he's come to know and care about. Hell, even the Chipped.

Micky exhales and shrugs. "You're right," he says and picks up the book. He slams it shut and slides it away on the floor. The book stops under the bed. "It's stupid. Let's play something else instead. Speaking of which," he looks at Sanna with wondering but amused eyes, "why on earth is Owena searching for needles?"

Sanna nods at the rabbit, who then hops across the floor, all the way to Sanna's feet. It rubs its chin against her toes. Sanna reaches out to pet its head. "It's something she read in a book."

"Another scary book?"

"No." Sanna lifts the bunny and places it on her lap. "More like a self-help book, I think. Owena says that we can poke a doll with needles, and if we think of a person really hard, they can feel the needles. Even if they are very far away."

Micky blinks rapidly, staring at Sanna's serious face. "That's terrible."

Holding the bunny against her chest, Sanna leans against the wall. "I think Nurse Saarinen needs some poking. What she's doing is not nice."

Nurse Saarinen. That's who the girls want to poke and torment. Of course. Considering what Owena and Sanna have gone through, Micky doesn't know if their evil plan is justified or not. Either way, it's not for him to decide.

Micky leans forward to pet the bunny, but it shies away from his touch, jumping down onto the floor. It hides behind Sanna's back.

"You need to let him come to you," Sanna says, smiling.

She turns slightly on her rear and focuses silently on something. Soon, the rabbit hops out of its hiding place and back onto Sanna's lap. Then, it makes its way over to Micky. The critter rubs its chin against his bent knee and puts its head down.

"Now you can pet him."

With a slow hand, Micky pets the creature's tiny, diamond-shaped head. Something about the silky hair and the rapidly wiggling nose soothes him.

"It's like you can talk to him," Micky says to Sanna.

Her brow furrowed, Sanna looks at Micky. "Of course I can talk to Mister Bun Bun. He's my best friend."

"Yes, yes, for sure." Micky smiles at her, then looks back down at the bunny. "But I mean actually *talk talk*. Like you can read his mind. Like we do while tapping."

She blinks and stares. Micky's not sure if Sanna's annoyed, confused, or angry. Nor does he understand why. But if he reads the girl right, pushing her with more questions would only make her withdraw again.

After a while, the rabbit gets up, stretching its plump body. Its yawn reveals two long, sharp front teeth. It hops over to Sanna and climbs back onto her lap. The girl chuckles and murmurs, "I know, right?"

"What?" Micky says, investigating Sanna and her pet. "I didn't hear you."

"I wasn't talking to you, Micky."

"Oh."

For several minutes, Micky watches the two and the undeniable connection between them. Mesmerized, he totally misses Owena walking back into the room, carrying a small box in her hands.

"Goodness!" Micky jumps on his seat. "You scared me."

"Why are you staring at Sanna and Mister Bun Bun?" Owena asks, in a matter-of-fact tone.

"Oh, I was just telling Sanna how cool it is that they're connected in this unusual way."

"What do you mean, unusual?" Owena asks, reaching for the doll. She sits down on the floor, opposite Micky and Sanna. She opens the small box and flips it over. Pins, thumbtacks, and needles pour onto the floor next to the doll's long, straw-like hair.

"Unusual means that—"

"I know what it means," Owena says. She spreads the doll's arms out on its sides. Calm and emotionless, she picks a pin from the floor and pokes the doll's hand with it, finally shoving it deep into the plastic. "But why do you think tapping is unusual? I thought all of you could do that. Not Mister Jenkins and Markus, but the rest of you."

Micky smiles and leans forward. He takes a needle and holds it up over the doll's foot. "You're right. We can all tap each other. Just not anim . . . " his words fade away. Astounded and confused, Micky sits back to lean against the wall. He watches Sanna and the rabbit with fresh eyes. "*Santa mierda*," he whispers. "You can tap animals?"

Sanna and the rabbit both look up at the same time; the girl is annoyed, and the bunny quickly drops its gaze back to the floor, alert and wide-eyed. He thumps his hind legs against the floor.

"Shh, Micky," Sanna whispers. "You're scaring him."

Micky's lost for words. Next to him, Owena pierces the doll's shoulder with a thumbtack. A handful of needles and pins poke out of the doll's small body.

"How long have you been able to tap animals, *niña*?

"Since we went back to the blue city."

Micky gets up from the floor and starts pacing around the circular carpet by the master suite's door. Should he go tell the others? What does this mean? Who else knows?

"Can . . . " He stops and stares at Sanna with wide eyes, wishing she'd look up and focus on him instead of the rabbit. "Can you show me how you do it?"

"Now you're just being silly, Micky." Sanna stretches her hoodie's front pocket, giving the rabbit an opening. The bunny nuzzles into her shirt, with only its round, fluffy tail poking out. "You just tapped me a while ago. You don't need tapping lessons from me."

"So you're saying that it's just like tapping people? When you talk to Mister Bun Bun?"

A shrug. Sanna's hands hug the lump under her shirt. "It's not so much me talking to him."

"No?"

"No. It's more like Mister Bun Bun talks to me."

Micky blinks in shock and shakes his head at his own question, even before he's asked it out loud. "In English?"

The girl glares at him in frustration. "Of course not in English. Animals don't speak the same language as we do. Micky, you're a grown-up. Why don't you know these things?"

"No one knew," Micky breathes out. "If they did, they would have . . . I don't know."

Sanna's eyes widen. "They would, what?"

"They'd . . . " Micky gives her an unsure look. "I don't even know. This is big. This is really big."

Sanna blinks and stares at him for a while. "You can't tell them."

Micky sits down on the bed, holding his head. After taking a few deep breaths, he leans his face against his hands, breathing through his fingers, eyes fixed on the bunny's fluffy tail. "Okay . . . okay."

"Okay, what?" Sanna pouts and wraps both of her arms around the lump that is Mister Bun Bun. "Micky, you're acting really strange."

"Yeah, Micky. Just come back here and poke Tina," Owena says, her eyes never leaving the doll. The pile of pins and needles on the floor is getting smaller and smaller. "Who cares about the stupid bunny?"

"Hey! Take that back, Owena." Sanna yells, her voice full of anger.

"Okay, whoa!" Micky gets up from the bed, raising his hands in the air, gesturing for a truce. "We all care about Mister Bun Bun. Obviously. He's part of the family."

Sanna nods. Owena, still lost in her strange task, doesn't say anything.

Micky reaches for the door handle. "I'm just going to pop downstairs and get another box of pins, okay?"

"*Micky*. You can't tell anybody!"

Sanna's rushed words stop Micky before he can sprint out of the room. He's desperate to talk this through with Bill.

"Not even Bill."

Oh mierda.

When Micky struggles to find his words, Sanna continues.

"They're grown-ups. And grown-ups ruin every-thing fun and important."

"I'm a grown-up," Micky says, feeling hurt, though he's not completely sure why. "I don't ruin fun and important things."

The stubbornness on her face turns into anger. "Then you don't tell anyone about Mister Bun Bun." Sanna's eyes are watery, and her fists close around the loose fabric of her hoodie.

"But I'm just saying—"

"No, Micky. Don't just say."

Sanna's words break Owena's focus. She looks up, first at Sanna, then at Micky.

"Okay, okay. Fine. I'm sorry." Micky sits down on the bed and buries his face back in his palms again. He's terrible at keeping secrets. The worst. How is he going to keep something this big from his friends downstairs? From Bill?

"Sanna is right," Owena says, inserting yet another needle into the doll's plastic torso. "If the grown-ups learned that Mister Bun Bun can talk, they'd just put him to work. It's much better if you don't tell anybody."

"To work?" Micky says, his voice unnaturally high. "Doing what exactly?"

"I don't know," Owena mumbles. "A lot of things."

"Without opposable thumbs?"

This question makes Owena look up from the doll. Her left eyebrow twitches. "What?"

Micky waves her off. He reaches for a pillow and hugs it against his stomach, a lot like Sanna is doing with the bunny. He can't tell this secret to Bill. To Maria. Kaarina. Definitely not Yeti. He does understand what Owena means by adults making animals work. And something deep within tells him that the fewer people who know about this communication skill, the safer Sanna's rabbit will be.

His sigh is half an exhale, half a cry.

"Micky?"

"Yes, Owena?"

"Are you sad?"

He looks up, still hugging the pillow. "No, I'm not sad."

"Are you upset?" Sanna asks with a quiet voice.

"Of course not, *niña*." He gives the girl a reassuring smile. "Just surprised, is all."

And worried I can't keep this secret for longer than five minutes.

"Here," Owena lifts a needle and points it in Micky's direction. "It's the last one. I'm giving it to you. Then Nurse Saarinen is toast."

"Toast?" Micky says.

Owena shrugs. "It's an old saying. People used food words in weird ways back then."

Without a single clear thought left in his mind, Micky walks over to Owena, sits down on the floor, and takes the needle from her. The doll is covered in sharp objects sticking out of its lifeless, plastic flesh. He should keep this little game to himself too. He doesn't want the girls to get in trouble. Yeti is suspicious enough when it comes to Owena and her strange, sometimes eerie ways.

Micky sticks the needle into the doll's right foot.

"You're not going to tell them?" Sanna asks, sliding closer to see the doll. Her other arm still wraps over her hoodie's pocket, protecting the bunny.

"I'm not going to tell them."

"Not even Bill?"

"Not even Beau, no."

Once out of pins and needles, Owena lifts the doll, investigating it closely. Then she lets it drop on the floor. "I'll go get some rope," she says, slipping away from the room before Micky can ask why. Then again—does he really want to learn what the rope is for?

A soft touch on his hand makes Micky turn around and look into Sanna's relieved eyes.

"Thank you, Micky. For keeping Mister Bun Bun's secret."

Micky smiles at Sanna. He lifts the doll from the floor and carefully holds it against his stomach, mirroring Sanna's gentle hold on the talking rabbit inside her shirt.

"No problem, *niña*. That's what family is for."

10

THE REVENANT

August 2089
Uploaded, The Egg

CHAPTER 1
LUNA

"And what does this thingy do?" Luna pokes at a glimmering white button that hovers in the air next to Doctor Solomon.

"Don't touch that."

"Why? What does it do?"

An annoyed murmur. That's the only answer Luna gets. Rolling her eyes at Solomon, Luna pokes the button a few more times. It shines white light and then shimmers down to a grayish color. With short, lazy steps, Luna walks around the space that looks and feels like a room but lacks everything that makes a room—well, a room.

Chairs and desks.

Picture frames and art.

Rugs and carpets.

It's all missing. There's no sign of a human living here. Luna stops roaming to stare at the woman in the white lab coat. It's not the first time the thought enters her mind, and surely it won't be the last.

Can Doctor Solomon still be considered a human? Can Luna?

Luna joins her new colleague with a slight shake of her head near a wall of transparent screens where zeros and ones flow seamlessly. Laura Solomon seems wholly lost in the screens. It's been a long time—a small eternity—since she's said anything but "Don't touch that," or "Give me a minute." But minutes turn to hours. Hours to . . . What exactly? Luna doesn't know. Such a deep-rooted concept doesn't seem to exist here.

Time.

"How am I still wearing the same clothes?" Luna asks out loud, knowing she won't get an answer but also desperate to change the track of her restless thoughts.

"Mm."

Annoyance and impatience fill Luna's entire being. Though there's no rush now—it's not like she's going anywhere—she wants answers. No, she *needs* them. And she needs them now.

What was supposed to be a dream job has turned into endless waiting on Luna's part. Just as Doctor Solomon had started to show Luna the lay of the land—how to operate in the egg—the doctor had gained access to a medical research folder of some sort, which she had thought was out of her reach. Annoyed by Laura's decreasing interest in teaching and training Luna the ropes, she hasn't asked what the folder was about. But Luna's sure it has something to do with Laura's former colleague and current adversary, Nurse Saarinen. No one else's work seems to devour Laura's mind like that of the woman who used to be her right hand.

She steps closer and leans in, her face close to Laura's. The woman's eyes are glazed over, the running numbers reflecting off them. How does she still have eyes? A face?

Luna keeps staring. After a while, Laura side-eyes her, breaking out of her trance. A deep breath. Her fingers stop moving in the air. "What? What do you want?"

Luna gives her a cheerful smile. "Oh, hey! You're back."

"You're pissing me off, Novak."

"Well, good."

Laura stares at Luna, her eyes now more human than a moment before. "It's not good," Laura says in her monotonous voice. "It's bad. Quite bad really."

"Um, excuse me," Luna says and blinks at Laura. "You invited me up here. I left my life as I knew it, and all my friends and allies, just to join you here. I'm not going to just stand around and watch you access more and more data and become more and more powerful. That was not the deal."

The breathtakingly beautiful woman turns her face and stares right at Luna, no emotion on her face. Laura's answer comes late, like there's a delay between them. "We'll continue with the training."

"When?"

Another delay. "In twenty minutes and thirty seconds."

Is she still accessing the files? While talking to Luna?

"Tell you what," Luna says, smiling at the doctor. "You answer three of my questions, and I'll leave you alone."

Laura's expression doesn't change. She doesn't even blink. Come to think of it, she never does. "Two questions. Yes or no answers."

"Sold."

Laura crosses her arms on her chest. A subtle movement above her brows tells Luna the doctor's waiting for her to ask her questions. Or maybe she just imagined the gesture. Either way, she'll finally learn something about this strange place.

"Why am I still wearing the same clothes as I was when I . . . well, died?"

Briefly, Laura looks upward and then back at Luna. "That's not a yes or no question."

Luna pouts and blinks. She knows she's acting like a five-year-old who's been told not to eat dessert before dinner. She also knows this kind of behavior will drive Laura bonkers in the long run.

"Fine." Laura walks past Luna and stops in the middle of the room. "You don't like your clothes?" She turns around and swipes the air. Another see-through screen opens. Three taps, and a flick of Laura's fingers—and Luna's missile-torn clothes turn into clean-white pants and a matching T-shirt. "There. Happy?"

Luna spreads her arms and looks down, scanning her new clothes. Soft, feather-light fabric moves with her seamlessly. They do feel like normal clothes, but also dreamlike. "Thanks," she says, extending her legs in front of her one at a time. "I guess."

"What's your second question?"

Luna looks up in awe. "But I didn't ask my first question yet."

"Sure you did. You wanted new clothes."

"No-oo," Luna says, extending the word. She stops fidgeting around in the skin-caressing fabric. "I said I wanted to know *why* I was still wearing the same clothes as I did before my upload. Besides . . . " Luna spreads her arms again and steps around, then faces Laura again. "I'd rather not look like a miniature you. Do you have anything black?"

Annoyance washes over Laura's face. With quick and somewhat hostile movements, she taps on the hovering screen again. Luna hurries to her, waving her hands in the air. "No, wait! That's not my second question."

Laura's finger freezes in the air. The smallest half-smile twitches her lips, but it's gone before Luna can sigh with relief. She leans her hands on her thighs and lets her head hang low. She feels like she should be out of breath, on the brink of an asthma attack, but her lungs work fine.

"The clothes you wear," Solomon says, "and the way you look . . . it's all created by your mind. A factory setting of sorts. A snippet of default code that you can build upon."

Luna looks up, her eyes clearing again as excitement washes away her frustration and worry. She can't wait to learn more about this place.

Solomon swipes away the hovering screen. She walks back to the wall filled with numbers and flickering lights and waves her hand in front of it. "All this you already know. Everything is accessible. All you need is to learn how to control it."

"How long did it take you? To learn it all?"

"I couldn't tell you. Weeks, maybe months. When I first arrived, all I saw was a white glow. It took me a while to build a system out of nothing and hack into cameras and sensors outside the egg. Once I figured it out, I thought months might have gone by."

"But it hadn't? It was just days?"

"Not days. Moments. Once I accessed the tile-road cameras in City of Finland, I could still see my body on the bench where I died. Nurse Saarinen's guards hadn't even reached me yet. That's when I realized I needed to learn how to control time as well. Or at least my perception of it. A million years could pass in here, while only a week went by outside the egg."

Luna opens her mouth to ask a question but quickly presses her lips back together. This time Laura's half-smile lingers a bit longer. She crosses her hands behind her back and continues to step around the egg.

"I know what you're about to say," she says to Luna, stopping by yet another white wall. After turning to face Luna, she gives her a quick smile. "But I already know how to control it," Laura says, imitating Luna's voice flawlessly. "I've been programming my whole life."

Luna swallows but doesn't say anything.

"But what you have to learn is to control your mind. You are the computer now. You are the code. And if you can't optimize your behavior to match what you are, you won't be able to do much of anything else either. Let that be your lesson one. No reason to move on with your training until you can do this one simple task."

Frowning, Luna lifts her chin. "I'm in control."

The doctor's laughter is brief and dry. Mocking. "Are you, now?"

"What is that supposed to mean?" Luna can feel the anger bubbling underneath her dreamlike skin. "There's nothing wrong with my . . . control panel. I can be a computer."

"Mm."

"Or an algorithm."

"Aha."

"Just put me to work. Show me the fucking ropes, and I'll fix everything that matters, and you can focus on your ridiculous clothes-changing magic tricks."

Laura's eyebrows rise. An actual smile on her face, she takes a few steps closer to Luna. "And tell me," her eyes narrow, "what's the first thing your omnipotent self would fix?" Laura raises her hand. "No, wait. Let me guess. You would . . . feed all the stray dogs on Earth? Or get your boyfriend patched up and out of the stasis capsule?"

Luna bites her lower lip, scanning the white space for objects. Any object will do. Just something to throw. Not at Laura, but against the wall. The rage of being misjudged burns in her mind. She can feel her face turning red, though when she looks at her reflection on one of the screens on the wall, she's just as pale as she was when she was still alive.

"I can fix shit," she says, her voice shaking. "Important shit."

Laura stares at her for a while. Her pause is long enough to make Luna squirm with anger and frustration. Finally, Laura exhales and turns back to her screens. With a lazy hand, she swipes the air, and another neon-blue screen opens. "What's your second question?"

Fuck you and your assumptions. That's what, Luna thinks. She closes her eyes, trying to calm herself by making her inhales and exhales the same length, just like Kaarina once taught her. She senses Laura's waiting gaze on her. As she opens her eyes, she tries a smile. It comes out as a crooked grin.

"Well?" Laura says in her usual sharp tone. "Anything else, or did you just want me to doll you up?"

Luna forces a smile. "Just one thing."

This time, Laura raises both her eyebrows.

"Do I get my own room, or am I stuck in this white hellhole with you for the rest of eternity?"

Rows and rows of servers, computers, CS-keys, screens, AR-glasses, and random widgets fill the tunnel-shaped room. The walls glimmer with the same unreal light that Doctor Solomon's egg does, only instead of a white glow, everything is purple.

"What is this place?" Luna asks, slowly moving her clinically white sneakers along the purple floor. "A server room?" She turns to face Laura. "I thought you said I wasn't ready for work yet?"

"I did. You're not."

"So why bring me here?"

Solomon walks into the purple space, spreads her hands, and turns around. "You wanted to see your room. This is it."

Mouth open, Luna stares at Laura in disbelief. "Let me get this right. You have limitless power over—well—everything. You can create new worlds, fix issues in any of them, and change my clothes by snapping your fingers . . ."

Laura shrugs. "And?"

"And you're putting me up in a storage room?"

Solomon's frown is not worried or angry. If anything, she looks puzzled. "It's not a storage room, Novak."

"Fine, a server room, then."

Laura shakes her head briefly.

Gesturing around the place, Luna scoffs and does her best not to raise her voice. "Then you must be seeing something different from what I'm seeing. Is that how this mindfuck of a place is going to work?

Guessing games? Is this some kind of a dynamic creative cloud version of the Rorschach inkblot test, where one person sees bunny ears and another a big fat—"

Doctor Solomon swipes the air, interrupting Luna's rant. After tapping twice on the keyboard, Solomon steps back. The light in the room remains purple, but all the technical devices disappear. Where the servers and CS-keys lined up just a second ago, a pack of dogs wags their tails, staring straight at Luna with their tongues hanging out.

"Better?"

Luna doesn't notice she's holding her breath until she takes a step closer to the virtual dogs. She needs to remind herself to exhale, then inhale again. Nothing in her body urges her to breathe. But her mind demands that she do so.

She bends over and extends her hand. Three dogs trot over, all circling her happily. Solomon stays further back, next to the door with white light glimmering underneath it.

"Your room, your reality. Make it whatever, and change it whenever."

Luna chuckles as one of the dogs sits in front of her and gives her a paw, then the other paw, then the first paw again. Her fingers caress the long fur, and just like her clothes, it feels real—just smoother. "You really thought I'd want to live among screens and gadgets?" she asks Solomon, all hostility now gone from her voice.

Luna can sense Solomon shrugging her shoulders better than she can see or hear it. "You are what you do. And you're a programmer. I thought that's what would make you feel at home."

After tousling the purple-yellow hair on the dog's head, Luna gets up from the floor and turns to face Solomon. "About that . . . " she waits for Laura to wave her off or tell her she's too busy to answer her questions. But the doctor just stares at her, a neutral look on her face. "If I really am just a program now, why do I still feel like I'm a human being?"

"Who said you're a program?"

Her annoyance returns. Luna closes her fists. Instead of arguing, she forces herself to wait for Laura to elaborate.

"You're not a program. You're the user. But now that you said it, maybe we made a mistake when creating a brain-mapping program which changes biochemical responses into mathematical ones. Things would be much simpler if people didn't have emotions. Don't you think?" Laura pauses to think, then waves Luna off. "Either way, I thought I explained this to you already."

"You—" Luna stops, closes her eyes, and takes a deep breath. She forces a small smile and speaks the words slowly. "With all due respect, Doctor Solomon, you haven't explained shit. All you've done is upload me to this strange-ass place, started teaching me what I can only call the basics—stuff I already knew— then told me to give you twenty minutes and thirty seconds, then tinkered with your shiny, see-through toys and completely forgot about my existence. If that's what I even do anymore."

"What?"

"Exist."

"Of course you exist. You are your mind. You are still here. Sure, the clothes, your body, and these surroundings are virtual reality, just bits of code that can be altered. But nothing here will change who you are as a person. Not if you don't want it to."

"And what the hell does that mean—" Luna waves Solomon off before she has time to answer. "You know what? Don't answer that. Just forget it. This is fine. All of this. Just . . . splendid. I think I'm done with this so-called training for now."

"Well, good." The doctor turns to leave. "Are we keeping the purple dogs?" Solomon asks, a trace of amusement in her voice.

Luna glances at her. "I'd prefer them to be a normal color, but whatever."

Two swipes, and all the purple color is gone. Yellow, brown, and brindle dogs run around the space. Natural yellow-white light fills the room.

"And a table would be nice," Luna says, still not looking at the doctor. She feels exhausted. Not sleepy exhausted, but like her mind is about to crash and burn.

A table appears in front of her. A few seconds later, a king-size bed with a golden frame.

"How about just a mattress on the floor?" Luna asks.

The golden bed disappears, and a simple mattress with a purple blanket and two hefty pillows appears. Luna walks over to it and carefully sits down. She runs her fingers cautiously on the sheets, as if they were about to vanish into thin air.

"All good?" Solomon asks, taking the last step between her and the glowing white door.

"What makes you think I like the color purple?" Luna asks. Suddenly, instead of feeling numb and emotionless like usual, she's restless. She feels eager to get back to work. Whatever that work might be.

"City of Serbia," Solomon says, in a matter-of-fact way.

"What about it?"

"The purple city. Again, I thought you'd feel more at home."

Luna investigates the doctor's face. Is Solomon mocking her? Does she really think that anything about City of Serbia would be something Luna wants to have in her life? Does this person know her at all?

Of course she doesn't, she thinks to herself. *She thought you'd like to sleep on a bed of servers and tablets.*

"I'll let you . . ." Doctor Solomon hesitates. "Rest? We can continue with the training once you feel more at ease with the surroundings." She opens the door and turns to leave.

"That's it? No fancy welcome dinner or fanfare?"

Laura lets her head hang for a moment before she looks over her shoulder. Her usual irritated expression has returned. "You want a party?"

Luna waves her off. "Just go. I'll see you tomorrow. If time still exists in this weird-ass place."

"We can count days, if you'd like. We can also alter your perception of time. There's no need to be bored here, just because it'll take you some time to learn the ropes."

"My . . . perception of . . ." Luna shakes her head and raises her hand, gesturing for Laura to forget about it. "Yeah, nope. Let's not. I'm not doing this right now. We'll talk *later*, once we continue with these lessons or whatever you call them. I'll have my shit together by then. Promise."

Some emotion Luna doesn't recognize washes over Laura's face, but it's gone before it ever really appears. Solomon turns and disappears into the white glow.

Luna lies down on the comfortable mattress. Hugging a pillow close to her chest, she closes her eyes. She wishes she could code herself to sleep—or whatever programs or users or code snippets do when they desperately need a break from a raging culture shock.

"You missed a spot."

Luna hovers by Doctor Solomon's shoulder, trying to keep up with the code running in front of her on a seemingly endless screen. Blue numbers run in front of her eyes, and though she's familiar with the code, Luna can't quite make sense of it.

"There, you did it again," she says to Solomon, pointing at a spot on the screen. A smaller keyboard opens where Luna's finger taps. Before she can start typing, Laura slaps at Luna's hand, then swipes her keyboard away.

"But that's City of Spain, isn't it?" Luna says, her hand twitching to point again. "If Margaret needs access to the building, you need to—" The second slap on her hand makes Luna jerk it back. "Ouch. No need to be so touchy. Just trying to help. Besides, wasn't this supposed to be my training time, not aggressive doctor stuck in a mindless flow time?"

Laura's fingers stop moving. She tilts her head from side to side, almost like rebooting to come back from the ocean of code. Sometimes it's like nothing about her is human, convincing Luna that they're both dead and trapped in some horrible loop. Then, Solomon shows the smallest gesture, a tiny sign of humanity.

A frown.

A brow twitching.

A faintly annoyed expression, tightening her unreal face.

Now, as Laura turns to face Luna, the white glow around them reflects off her eyes, making the woman in a white coat look more like a computer than a human.

"Lewis will have her access. But I'd prefer it if Nurse Saarinen didn't see her coming."

"Right." Luna forces herself to focus on the task at hand. "Margaret is not one to fuck things up. If you want to give her access to the building, why don't you just . . . " Luna moves closer, dodging Laura's hands, gesturing for her to leave the wall alone. Luna swipes the air, and the small keyboard reappears. She starts typing. "Just get camera access and scan Nurse Saarinen's movements over the last, I don't know, a month? Two months?"

"Negative." Laura reaches past Luna and swipes her keyboard away. "The virus protection will inform her of someone trying to access her database. The last thing we need is for her to become suspicious. If she moves the test subjects, it'll be that much harder to find them again."

Luna cocks her head. "They have names, you know. Margaret's family. Mindy and Meredith."

Doctor Solomon shrugs and mumbles something about "too many M's," but Luna can't make sense of her low murmur. She sidesteps and pokes another spot on the wall. A platform of buttons appears.

Neat.

Just as she's about to press the green button with random numbers on it, Laura's hand taps on the wall, and the buttons disappear.

Asshole.

"Didn't I tell you not to touch anything?"

"Yeah, but you also told me you'd train me so I can help you."

"And I will."

"Yeah, but when? All you've done today is teach me more basics, then ignore me for a small eternity, leaving me alone with some bullshit video like I'm a five-year-old."

Laura takes a deep breath, her eyes flickering back to the wall. It's clearly hard for her to break away from it, even for a second. "Okay, you're right. The video was bullshit."

Luna crosses her arms. "And chips and dip? What kind of a shitty-ass diet do you think I live on?"

"You don't need a diet," Solomon says, looking over Luna's shoulder. "Not here."

"Then why feed me at all?"

"It's part of the process."

"The process of what exactly? Last I checked, I'm already dead. All out of extra hearts, killed by the level ten boss."

Laura stares at her, a blank look on her face.

"Video games?" Luna's brow furrows. "Nothing? Don't you have a kid who likes games?"

Doctor Solomon takes another deep breath while something dark washes over her face.

Shit. Bad comment. Erase, erase.

"Scratch that," Luna says hurriedly. "Never mind."

Funny how annoyance and sometimes humor or even compassion, have served to pull Laura back into her human form.

After an extended, awkward moment, Laura turns toward the wall, opens a row of switches, and flicks two of them on. Two white chairs appear out of thin air. After watching Laura safely sit down on hers, Luna follows her example and takes a seat. She crosses her legs and hands, trying to look as innocent and worry-free as possible. As much as Solomon's lack of commitment to her training annoys Luna, she still needs her—more than she's ever needed anyone in her life.

Or is it her afterlife?

"The buttons you were about to mess with are stasis capsules in various AR-cities. The numbers are chip ID's, stating who's inside, and the colors go with the cities the capsules are in."

"So you can open the capsules from here?" Luna asks, her eyes wide and her voice breathless. "And whoever's inside gets out safely?"

"Sure, I can open them." Laura shrugs a shoulder. "But why bother? Everyone essential is already released."

Because it's the right thing to do, you sick, sadistic—

"Save your anger, Novak."

"What?"

"I know what you're thinking."

The fuck you do.

"You think that everyone in the capsules should be released because it's the right thing to do."

Luna rolls her eyes. "Right. You can read my mind. Go figure."

Laura cocks her head ever so slightly. "Don't be foolish. I'm not Unchipped. But I don't need to be. Not to predict what goes on inside your head."

"Oh, so now I'm easily predictable?"

Solomon nods. "And naïve."

Luna's hands grab a hold of the chair's edges. Her face twitches as she tries to keep her expression as neutral as possible.

"And you have severe anger issues."

"I do not—" Luna starts, her voice loud and shaky. She presses her lips into a thin line and closes her eyes.

One, two, three, four . . . how is this supposed to . . . five, six . . . fucking calm me . . . seven . . . down . . .

"Not to mention that you're impulsive and make extremely poor judgment calls when it comes to people."

Bouncing off her seat, Luna grabs the chair and tosses it toward the door that leads to her room. Her scream comes out weak, like it's muffled by water or some weird, invisible jelly. The chair disappears into the white glow with a dull *thump* sound. Out of breath, Luna turns to stare at Doctor Solomon, eyes drilling into her expressionless face.

"You don't know shit about me."

"Sure I do."

Luna shakes her head. "You don't know the first thing about—"

"I know you grew up in Belgrade in an average family where you were never expected to thrive at anything. I know you took on programming because numbers have always made more sense to you than people. You feel like you can control them. Just like animals. Being in control is the very reason why you surrounded yourself with wild animals after The Great Affliction."

"Dogs are nothing like numbers."

"But wild animals are. They have clear rules and pecking orders. No surprises, no disappointments." Solomon crosses her arms and leans back on her chair. "I know you think you love this stasis capsule boy, Jovan, despite your conflicted feelings during your final moments. And my mother has talked enough about him for me to know that he's just as hopeless as you are when it comes to excelling in the world. You two and your little stunt back in United Inland completely derailed the black market's plans to take over City of Finland." Laura shakes her head. "A second chance for those who so mightily want to live outside the Happiness-Program—ruined. And for what?" Solomon's eyes narrow. "A lovers' quarrel."

"That's not . . ." Luna's rage starts to turn into confusion. Is that what happened? Did they really do that? "We never—"

"But Laura, we were in love," Laura again mimics Luna's voice. "So foolish. This thing you call *love* is nothing but hormones, dopamine, and brain chemistry, pulling your leg—or should I say brain. And now that I've told you this, you'll just get angrier and insist that I'm wrong."

Just because you don't know how to love—

"And then you're going to try and insult me by telling me that I'm too cold-hearted or what's the word you like to use . . . ah, yes, *clinical* to know what love is."

Well, fuck.

Laura leans forward, her elbows pressed against her knees and fingers crossed in a relaxed manner. "You will take all of this personally. Especially the way I read you with such ease, like you're just one code among others. Well, Novak, I've got news for you." Solomon's smile is almost sincere. "That's because you are."

Grunting in frustration, Luna throws her hands in the air, pacing around in a small circle. She pulls her hair and stops to stare at the spot where her chair had disappeared. "What the hell is the meaning of this? Huh? Any of it? Why did you upload me up here in the first place if I'm such a waste of your time and memory space?"

A click and a swoosh echoes next to Luna. When she turns around, a new white chair—maybe the very same chair she threw into nothingness—stands next to her. She takes a seat, crosses her arms and pouts, looking away from her rude and heartless mentor.

"You're here because of those things. Everything that I just said."

A brief, mocking laugh escapes Luna's lips. Then she scoffs, still looking away.

Laura says, "Because you never found meaning in humanity, you lost yourself in numbers. Code. Programs. You never had the kind of life you would have enjoyed and chosen for yourself, and so you focused on educating yourself about programming."

Luna turns her head slowly, too baffled to feel outraged. This woman. This *thing*. How dare she?

Solomon investigates Luna's face. After a moment of silence, she sighs and leans back in her chair. "Let's try this. How does it make you feel if I tell you that I uploaded you because of your above-average intelligence?"

Luna raises her eyebrows. "A hell of a lot better than your earlier rude-ass annihilation of my whole existence."

"Mm. And how does it make you feel if I tell you that it's good to have a strong personality? That what most would see as your weaknesses, are in fact your utmost strengths?"

Luna bites her lower lip. The rage is gone, but the confusion still persists. "Go on."

"Jovan is your key to happiness. You now realize that whatever fight you two were in the middle of when you died doesn't matter. The dogs show that you're a pure person who can love and care for other beings, even if it's in a unique, misunderstood way."

Luna leans forward in her chair. Something warm burns her eyes, and she has to swallow hard to keep the feeling to herself.

Don't you dare cry. You're an algorithm. Ones and zeros don't cry.

Laura's smile deepens. "Feeling better?"

Luna meets her gaze. Solomon's words have released the pressure in her throat and chest. All anger has vanished. For the first time since she arrived in the egg, she feels whole. Almost normal. Maybe this place isn't that bad after all. Maybe if she just finds patience and lets Laura guide her—

"Well, it's all lies. You're feeling better because of a load of crap I just poured down your throat."

Luna's head jerks back in surprise.

Motherfucker.

"What the hell is wrong with you?"

Laura gets up and walks to the wall. She taps on a few screens and lowers her chin to investigate a gadget of some sort. "It's not me who needs to be fixed."

"I'm not your fucking rescue dog!"

"Mm."

Luna bounces up and marches over, placing herself between Doctor Solomon and the see-through wall.

"We're not done yet. We barely started, and you've already ditched me several times to tinker with your magical buttons and switches!"

A deep sigh. Laura takes a step back and tilts her head, crossing her arms. For a moment, they just stare at each other, Luna fuming and the doctor looking as bored as ever.

"What do the stasis capsule buttons do?" Luna asks, focusing on the tone of her voice. If she wants Laura ever to teach her anything, she needs to stay calm. Collected. *Emotionless*.

"You can talk to them."

Luna takes a sharp breath in, her eyes wide and fixed on Laura. "The people in stasis?"

A shrug. "The Chipped ones, yes."

Luna's body feels too calm, too static for the rush of emotions washing through her. Her heart should be skipping. Her legs should turn to jelly. She should be holding her breath, and the room should start spinning around her. But none of that happens. She just stands silently, her thoughts racing back to the person.

Jovan.

Despite the hurt Luna feels when the images of Jovan and Vesna flicker through her mind, she would give anything to be able to talk to him again.

Like a reflex, Luna peeks over her shoulder at the space where the buttons appeared. Laura catches her gaze, even before Luna's feet start twitching toward the magical buttons.

"Forget it. It's not a good idea."

Luna stops and stares at Laura. She lifts her chin, and without looking away, she swipes at the wall with her left hand. A row of switches and a keyboard appear, but no buttons.

Doctor Solomon drops her head and rubs the bridge of her nose. A rare moment, seeing this simple human gesture from her. "That's not the right server, Novak. Just leave it. I'll show you how to contact Iris or Mrs. Salonen instead."

Luna sidesteps and swooshes her arms around. A screen with a cityscape appears. Orange lights glimmer in the night. Numbers and letters flicker to life by the high buildings, tile roads, and landscape. A cursor appears in front of her. Luna lifts her hands and looks for a keyboard, but just as she locates one, Laura taps on the cityscape twice and pushes the image to the side. It disappears with a swooshing sound. "I said, do not touch that."

"That was City of Maine, wasn't it?"

"You'll just make a mess," Laura murmurs, ignoring Luna's question.

It's not Jovan's capsule, but suddenly Luna's obsessed. What were the numbers for? The letters? Does Laura have satellites to spy on the cities? The thought hits her hard. She blinks, taking deep breaths even though there's nothing wrong with the airflow in her lungs.

"You have . . . access? To the cities?"

"Of course I do."

"Is it just satellites and cameras? Can you actually touch things?"

Solomon's brief laugh is dry. "Last I checked, my opposable thumbs are buried six feet under at the rapeseed field by City of Finland's Chip-Center."

"But you . . . "

"I could dig myself up? Activate my chip and return from the dead?"

"Well . . . " Luna bites her lower lip, unsure what to think or feel. "Could you?"

"This is the perfect example of why you're not ready."

Chin an inch higher, Luna swallows down her anger. "Ready for what?"

"Your training." Laura straightens her perfectly straight lab coat sleeves and picks imaginary lint off her arm. "You accuse me of teaching you what you call *the basics*, and at the same time you keep simplifying and mystifying everything. Resurrection, zombies, and robots. That's what's rushing through your pretty little head right now?"

Yes.

"No."

A knowing smile lingers on the doctor's lips, but her annoyance covers it nearly perfectly. "And when I tell you that we have access to people in stasis, that we can talk to them as long as their chips are intact, what's the first thing that you want to do?"

Whatever. You cold-hearted, rotting, dead-inside, piece of—

"Oh, save me from your dirty looks, and I'll save you from pointing out the obvious."

I'm obvious? Fine, at least I'm not a selfish asshole in a lab coat—

"And before you start calling me names and taking everything I say personally, stop and think." Laura taps her temple, narrowing her eyes. "Think, Novak. Why are you here, and not pushing up daisies with your worm-filled body, somewhere in the ruins of United Inland?"

Luna closes her eyes. The anger makes it hard to focus. Her hurt feelings make it hard to follow Doctor Solomon's train of thought. But if she won't listen to her, do as she's told . . . then what chance does Luna ever have to learn about this new world she's now part of?

"You uploaded me because you needed my help."

Laura nods slowly. "Correct. And what is it I need your help with?"

"Code. Programs. Finding . . ." Shit, of course. "Rescuing Margaret's family before Nurse Saarinen kills them."

Now her smile is obvious. Laura makes small circles with her hand, gesturing for Luna to continue.

"If I call someone in stasis, it should be someone whose life is in danger. Not Jovan." Luna pauses to stare into the white nothingness. "To help you, I need to start thinking like a computer, not like a human being."

"Bingo." Laura turns and wipes her hands together, then looks up the wall. "And that's the end of today's lesson. Why don't you go play with your purple strays, and we'll pick this up again at a later time?"

"But I want to help. Besides, it was me who told you where Meredith and Mindy are hidden in the first place, remember? Without Jovan, we wouldn't have learned about this off-radar Chip-Center in City of Spain. We would be still looking for a microchip in a sea of . . ." Luna makes a big gesture with her hand, "I don't know, a sea of other microchips, or something."

"Mm." Laura's focus is back on the code that runs along the wall.

"Okay, I know that didn't make a lot of sense, but listen." Luna steps to the wall and swipes at a random spot. A cursor appears with a white, glimmering box.

This shit is so cool.

She swooshes the cursor away and swipes again. This time, a green tile road with people walking on it appears.

Swipe.

Swipe.

Swipe.

She opens new screens and views until the wall has tripled in size. Finally, a row of neon-colored buttons appears. Just as Luna's about to press one of them, Laura's hand blocks hers.

"I don't like to repeat myself, Novak."

"But have you talked to Mindy? What's the plan? Is Margaret already in City of Spain?"

Laura turns away from Luna and starts closing down the screens and keyboards she's opened.

"Is Bill going to attack Nurse Saarinen?"

Doctor Solomon scoffs and gives Luna a quick, amused look. Without bothering to answer Luna's question, she keeps cleaning the wall.

"Fine, maybe not Bill. But Maria? Yeti?"

"Novak. Go to your room."

A quick rush of anger washes through her. "I am not your kid, Laura. You can't just kill me and then send me to my room like I'm five."

"It wasn't me who killed you."

Luna's scream sounds strangely soft, the egg's white walls muffling the sound.

"Yell all you want," Solomon says. "But I'm hardly the one to blame for the missile attack."

Luna kicks the chair hard, but all she gets is a dull *thud*. The chair moves a few feet over and lands softly on its side.

"And I'm well aware that you're not my child. One stubborn, immature daughter is enough for me. Although, I don't remember Sanna ever giving me this much trouble—"

"Sanna's eleven years old, Laura. She's supposed to be immature. You'd know this, if you weren't such a fucking lousy mother!" Luna yells, her nails drilling into the palms of her hands. It should hurt her, but it doesn't. "You used her as a test subject, then abandoned her. That's right, I know all about it. Kaarina told me. All that kid ever had was a freaking rabbit and a slight chance of hope because she got away from you. But did you let her enjoy her freedom or the people who actually cared about her? No, no! Not the great Laura fucking Solomon. All you care about is power and being omnip—"

Luna's lips keep moving, but her voice is gone. She stops waving her hands and stomping her feet. Panic enters her brain as her fingers feel for her lips. Still there. Moving, but not a single sound comes out. At the top of her lungs, she screams once. Then again. No sound. Nothing.

What fresh hell is this?

Laura sits down on her chair, crossing her legs, then her arms. Lips pressed into a thin line, she looks at Luna but doesn't say a word. The dull expression on her face is still there, but another emotion is mixed in now.

Hurt.

Luna's words have hurt her, and though she's not showing much of it, the pain is immense enough for Luna to see. Great and powerful, sure. But even Doctor Solomon has a weak spot—something she seems to regret.

She stops her silent screaming. She stops pacing around, lets go of the hair she's been pulling. Tears of anger should blur her eyes, but Luna's not sure if crying is even an option here. Or, if it is, would Laura put an end to that too? Just as fast as she silenced Luna's temper tantrum?

Luna walks over to the toppled chair, picks it up, and sits down. The chair is placed far away from Solomon, next to a wall with no screens, buttons, or keyboards. When Luna looks around the space, she notices all of it has vanished. Only the white, endless glow surrounds them.

Luna buries her face in her hands. Her elbows dig into her thighs as she sits and calms her raging mind, taking deep breaths. Tears should be falling, she knows. She's crying on the inside, but nothing wet reaches her eyes. She breathes even deeper, matching the length of her inhales with her exhales. If only she could hear these breaths in her ears. That might soothe her. Or maybe not. Maybe nothing will.

For a short eternity, she sits with her closed eyes. Laura Solomon's lab coat doesn't rustle, nor does her shoe tap against the white floor. No sighs, no clearing her throat, no words.

I shouldn't have said those things to you, Luna thinks, but can't bring herself to look up and try to say the words out loud. *I'm sorry.*

Almost as if she can read Luna's mind, Laura gets up from her chair. Soft but strong steps echo around the egg, as she makes her way to Luna. What is she going to do? Slap her? Leave her on mute forever?

Swoosh.

Luna looks up from her hands. A black and white button shines in front of her, with the letter F and number 33 above it. "What is that?" she says, startled to hear her own voice again.

"A stasis capsule. One of Ef's in United Inland."

Luna stares at the button, her mind suddenly blank.

"You wanted to call him." Solomon shrugs. "Call him. Just be warned, his chip will be integrated with the egg and your manifestation here. Meaning, he'll see everything around you. He'll be able to see through your eyes and read your mind." Laura turns to walk away.

Luna's hand shakes, hovering over the button.

"And Novak." Without moving her hand away from the button, Luna looks over at Doctor Solomon's hardened face. "That's the last time you *ever* speak a single word about my daughter."

CHAPTER 2
JOVAN

"You really said that to her?"

Jovan watches as Luna fixes the pillow under her head. Two dogs lie against her legs, and the room glows with a pleasant, natural-yellow light.

"I did, but I sort of wish I hadn't."

It's good to hear her voice. Luna can't see him, stuck in the stasis capsule, but Jovan can see Luna's surroundings as they talk. She said this is something that Doctor Solomon calls "visiting."

"Sounds like she had it coming," Jovan says. "Her whole act, calling people 'dear' and 'sweetie,' never really fooled anyone in the first place. And now she's supposedly on our side? Why? Just because she has a daughter among the rebels? I'm telling you, the woman is cold and cruel. And this proves that she's still just that. Her telling you all those things about your life and pointing out your, um . . ."

55

"Shortcomings," Luna says when Jovan hesitates. It's hard for him to say anything negative about her character. After all he's done, after his betrayal . . . he's amazed Luna's called him in the first place. For now, all they've done is focus on the comfort that being able to talk with one another brings. But a gloomy, invisible memory looms between them. A lump of regret. It's present in the space between them, but both of them are carefully avoiding addressing its existence. He wishes they could go back to how things were before. Before he made his fatal mistake and entered the red room in the remote AR-resort with Vesna—ruining everything that was important in his life . . .

Jovan forces the thoughts aside. "Right," he says, "Sounds like Solomon has no problem hitting you below the belt."

"True. But Solomon did it for a reason. It's all part of my training."

"Training? For what exactly?"

"To be a machine. To accept that I'm no longer human."

"That's . . . But that's not really true. Is it?" Jovan feels a need to swallow, to shake his head, something to get the unpleasant rush of thoughts to stop. Something to keep the lump further away. "I thought you said you're still, well, *you*?"

"Jovan, it's an exaggeration," Luna says hurriedly, but uncertainty shadows her voice. "It's just buttons and switches and code snippets. I really don't have the words to describe it. Not yet, at least. All of this . . . It's a whole different ball game from the programming I'm used to. But hey, enough about me. How are you holding up in there? Do you know where you are located? Who you're with?"

Jovan forces his mind to accept Luna's clumsy attempt to change the topic. She sounds like she cares. Truly. But there's something hesitant in her voice that she clearly tries to hide. They can both feel the lump between them grow. "What, being stored inside a lab tube, naked and hairless?" Jovan manages to keep his voice soft and somewhat carefree. "You've been in stasis yourself. Hard to imagine you'd forget what it's like?"

Luna pauses to consider this. "It must be different for everybody. Like dreams and dreaming. We all experience certain things in a unique way."

"What makes you say that?"

"Because I don't remember a thing from it," Luna says, frowning. "Just the moment when I woke up and Jafari pulled me out."

Jovan stays quiet for a while. Will he forget all this, too? Once he's healed enough for Ef's crew to remove him from the capsule?

"It's strange, though," he finally says. "Time has sort of . . ." He searches for the right word. "Well, it hasn't stopped. But it's like . . ."

"Like time never existed in the first place?"

Jovan laughs briefly. "So you do remember."

"I don't."

Jovan looks through Luna's eyes and around the unreal space she's in. A tunnel-shaped room glows dimly, and on top of the bed, a pack of dogs snoozes away with Luna tucked in the middle. When Luna reaches over to scratch one of them, the dog lifts his head, tilting it, like he's asking Luna a question.

Caressing the dog's head, Luna shrugs. "It's just that it's the same. Up here. With time."

"Oh."

What else can he say? The place Luna's in is way beyond his brain capacity. He can barely comprehend what's happening to himself at the moment; being in a stasis capsule, the nanobots nurturing him back to life after a missile attack that tore parts of his body to pieces.

All he wants is to go back in time. To tuck himself and Luna into a tent in the middle of the wasteland. Snuggle up to keep warm. Tell bad jokes and write the red rooms out of existence.

"Lu?"

"I'm here," Luna answers quickly and gestures around her. "I mean, neither of us is going anywhere anytime soon, I think."

"About what happened with Vesna—"

"Let's not talk about it," she says hurriedly. "Not now. I'm . . . I'm not ready for that. Vesna, the missiles, the egg . . . it's too much."

They both fall silent for a while, each lost in thought.

"Do you remember when you got trapped in that crater on the road?"

"I said that time doesn't exist here," Luna answers. "I didn't say that I've forgotten the past."

"So you do remember?"

"Of course I remember the crater. What about it?"

If clearing his throat was possible, that's what Jovan would do—twice or three times—to buy some time. But he's already started to ask the question.

"Did you mean what you said? Back then?"

"About feeding you and Jafari to stray dogs if you wouldn't help me up? You bet your ass I did."

"No, not that." Jovan stares at the dog Luna's fingers are caressing. "About loving me?"

Her fingers stop on the dog's head. The canine lifts his head, again looking like a question mark. Then Luna keeps on stroking the long, brown hair, never answering Jovan's question.

"I'm sorry, Lu, I just—"

"Don't do that."

"Do what?"

"Apologize."

"I didn't mean to make you feel—"

"Don't do that either."

Jovan stutters to find the words, swallowed in a tide of regret.

"Don't tell me how I'm feeling. You have no idea."

"You're obviously—"

"I'm not obvious!" Luna's sudden snap startles two of the dogs, but the rest keep snoozing away on the bed. Are they programmed to not react to loud noises? "I'm so sick and tired of people telling me what and who I am. How I feel and why. That love is just a bunch of hormones and chemicals swarming in my brain."

"Whoa, hey, I never said that. That's a load of horse shit."

Luna sits up on the bed, her fists wrapped around a purple pillow. "Is it, though?"

Again, Jovan has no words. And on the other hand, that's all he has at the moment. *Focus, egghead.* It's the memory of his beloved friend, Dunja's, voice, scolding him. *Use your brainy words.*

"I don't think we really understand things like love enough to put a label on them," he says. Luna's grip on the pillow loosens. Instead of arguing, she waits for Jovan to elaborate. "I mean, we can hardly understand what happens to our minds when we dream. Or what happens to us when we die. Hell, last I checked, they can't even tell what makes an Unchipped person an Unchipped person."

"HSP," Luna says, burying her face between her arms. "It's something to do with being a highly sensitive person."

Jovan blows air through his lips. Or tries to—no sound comes out. "A what now?"

"That's what it said in Doctor Solomon's notes. I may not be able to figure out all her shiny new toys up here, but I can still access some files and folders when I'm left alone watching a bad introduction video like a half-dim teenager. I mean, chips and dip? What does she think I am, a junk food addicted child?"

"Lu, you're losing me. What video? And there's *food* up there?"

"Jovan, there's *everything* up here. You can smell, feel, touch, taste, hear . . . It's not like being dead at all. Actually, it's the opposite."

He considers this. Tries to understand this.

"I can create a room with a few clicks of a button. I can go back in my memories and watch them—relive them. Solomon can make the time go faster or slower. She can mute everything, so there's no sound. I'm pretty sure she can freeze everything around her too, but I'm hoping I won't get a confirmation of that."

Nothing she says makes sense. None of it.

"Jovan? Did I lose you?"

"No." He feels the urge to shake his head. "Never. No, I'm here. I just . . ."

"You still don't get it?"

"None of it. I'm sor—"

"Don't."

"Sorry. I mean . . . shit."

Luna sighs and climbs up from the mattress. "I mean, of course you don't get it. Even *I* don't get it. Just a small fraction of this place makes sense to me." She walks over to a door, under which a white light gleams. "All she's given me is this . . . " A few swipes and a see-through screen with a cursor appears in front of Luna's face. She starts tapping on it, numbers running through the air. "What if I told you I could take us back . . . " She taps and swipes. "Here."

Green, rolling fields open around them. Luna turns around, slowly, to show Jovan the scenery through her eyes.

Lush trees.

Scorching sun.

Coffee mugs next to a backpack.

A notebook, forgotten at the front of a tent for two.

"Is this a live feed?" Jovan asks, devouring the national park where he once felt freer than he'd ever felt in his life.

"No, ding-dong. This is a memory. My memory, reflected on a screen and played like a movie. See . . . " She walks closer to the tent. Through the half-open zipper door, two pairs of bare feet stick out—a woman's and a man's.

"That's us?"

Luna smiles and rolls her eyes. "It's either us or we're stalking some other couple having sex in the middle of the Serbian countryside."

Jovan stares at the scene. He can feel her touch on his skin, the way Luna's long, brown hair tickles his chest and face. The way she curls her toes around his to keep warm. It's not just her memory. It's his as well.

"Lu, what Solomon said about love being numbers or whatever, I just don't buy it. Because even now, with you stuck up there and me here, I still feel different when I'm with you. No matter how badly I fucked up, I still feel like we're connected in a way that no one else can understand."

Luna sits down in the green grass, her fingers brushing through the long straws. "I know. I feel it too."

"Luna, I love—"

"Okay, love birds, time to wrap it up."

Doctor Solomon's piercing voice startles them both. Luna jumps up and spins around. Jovan stares at the woman in her white lab coat and matching shoes. Her blond hair is up in a ponytail, and though he can see she's a middle-aged woman, somehow she looks . . . *ageless*.

"I need you in the grid, Novak."

"The . . . what now?" Luna swipes the air, and the peaceful green forest vanishes into thin air. One of the dogs jumps off the bed and hurries to Luna's side. She pats its head distractedly.

"No time to explain. We've located Nurse Saarinen. Margaret is outside the secret base right now. We need access to the facility cameras to know what we're dealing with."

Luna's face turns serious. "Security cameras. Drones?"

Solomon nods.

"That I can do. Just give me a CS-key, and I'm on it."

Solomon turns and walks out of the room into a white glow. When Luna follows, Jovan is temporarily blinded by the white nothingness that glimmers all over.

The two women cross the unreal space where another door, rimmed by white light, appears in front of them.

"You're thinking with your old brain again," Solomon says. With her hand on the door handle, she turns to face Luna. All Jovan can do is stare. Laura Solomon is unnaturally beautiful. God-like.

"There are no CS-keys here, Novak. You have to stop thinking in such an elementary way."

Luna spreads her hands and lets them drop to her sides. "Fine. No more plastic and wire and blinking lights. But switches and magical buttons?"

The stunning creature shakes her perfect head. The shimmering halo around her ponytail seems to brighten.

"Okay, no magic buttons." Luna huffs. "What then?"

For the first time since Jovan set eyes on Doctor Solomon, he sees a genuine, almost childlike smile appear on her face.

Excitement.

Joy.

Challenge.

All the emotions linger in that smile as she opens the door and lets Luna walk in.

"This."

A space that is more like a balcony than a room with four walls opens around the two women. As Luna walks across the space and stops by the edge, Jovan struggles to make sense of what he is seeing. Too baffled to ask questions, he waits for Luna to circle back around to Solomon, who is standing in the middle of the mind-bending balcony, spinning around and tapping floating screens and keyboards.

Luna kneels down and holds onto the edge of the white flooring. She peeks over the cliff; it's black, yet somehow glowing, as far as Jovan's—or Luna's—eyes can see. Mesmerizing. Tempting. When she looks up and onto the horizon, the same glow continues like a never-ending darkness. But down there, it's different. Eternal, somehow.

"Okay, so the view is pretty impressive," Luna says, clearly trying to sound calm and collected. But Jovan can feel that inside, she is just as overwhelmed as Jovan is. "But I don't get it. You have tons of that going on inside." Luna gestures at the screens and hovering objects around Solomon. "What's so special about this space?"

Though she's facing Luna, Solomon doesn't stop tinkering with her screens or look at Luna when she speaks. "Inside? That's just the front end."

"And this is, what, the back end?" Luna asks and crosses her arms. "You're the one who told me to stop thinking in a such a . . . what's the word you used?"

"Elementary."

"Right. That. And now this? This is just . . . just too simple."

This time Solomon's hand freezes midair. Her unnaturally blue eyes fixate on Luna. "Having access to every single computer, database, algorithm, and server in the world is *too simple*?"

Luna spreads her hands, squirming under Solomon's gaze. "I didn't mean simple, *simple*"—she makes quotation marks with her fingers—"just that I expected something . . . fancier."

Solomon's expression remains neutral. Bored. Like she's dealing with a drunken neighbor who won't stop knocking on her door to tell her the sky is still blue. That sort of thing happened to Jovan, back in the day when Belgrade was still Belgrade, and the only reality that existed.

Luna clears her throat. "No offense." She turns around and points her hands at the black space opening in front of them. "This grid, or whatever, is pretty neat. And having access to everything definitely sounds tempting. But don't you think it lacks something?" She turns to face Laura again. "Something like—"

"Say robots, and I'll push you off the cliff before you can finish that sentence."

Luna's mouth pops open. Instead of horror, wonder and surprise fill her voice. "So there is gravity here then?"

A muffled scoff escapes Solomon's lips. Every time Jovan's convinced of the doctor not having an inch of humanity left in her, she shows some small trace of emotion. Mostly irritation, but human nonetheless. "Of course there's gravity, Novak. How else do you think you're able to stick to that absurd mattress of yours? Hmm? Or the dogs? Do you see them floating around? No. Real dogs don't fly."

Are they real, though? Jovan wants to ask, but he's too afraid to interrupt Luna's train of thought. It seems the woman has forgotten he's still here, listening in. Learning about this new world.

Slowly, Luna walks back to the cliff. She kneels down again and lets her arm hang over the edge like she's dipping her fingers into the ocean. "Was it like this when you first arrived?"

Solomon sighs. She keeps tapping open views of a multicolored city with low buildings and old-fashioned roads. In the middle, a familiar-looking building blazes in the midday sun. Jovan's been there before, a long time ago. City of Spain, but when it still was called something else. Just a small town off the coast of southern Spain. He's forgotten what it was called but will never forget what he and Dunja found downstairs in the construction yard. Back then, he had no idea what the tubes and wires were for. Now, he's in one, as they speak.

Luna pokes Solomon's shoulder. The doctor's whole body freezes. Slowly, she turns her face toward

Luna, her voice filled with threat and authority. "Did you just *poke* me?"

Luna takes a step back. "Well, you wouldn't answer my question." She clears her throat to cover for the fact that her voice shakes.

The pause is awkwardly long. Luna doesn't move. The usually vibrating air, the silence, even the open screens in front of them seem to have frozen.

Just as Jovan is about to scream with tension, Solomon's smooth voice echoes around them again. "An empty space. That's all there was when I first arrived."

"And what came first? The egg or the . . ." Luna turns a bit to gesture to blackness behind them.

"The egg is my room. My space. The computers and programs, they're all still down on Earth, or the place that you call your own reality. We have access because we are, in fact, inside the same computer."

"Where is the computer?"

Solomon shrugs and continues to tap on the City of Spain landscape. "Everywhere."

"So this place is just . . . what?" Luna asks. "Folders and files?"

"Now who's being overly simple?" Solomon taps and swipes. A microphone icon and three white dots appear next to her white lab coat. "It's my mind. And yours."

Knowing very well that it's scientifically impossible, somehow Jovan still feels dizzy and slightly nauseated.

"So if this is your mind as well as mine, how are we seeing the same—"

Luna's question is interrupted by a muffled sound. "Hello? Doctor Solomon?"

Jovan knows this voice well. He'd recognize it in his sleep.

"Yes, Iris. I'm here. Is my mother there with you?"

"She is."

"Good. Let's get this over with, so I can work on something less tedious."

Luna cups her mouth in surprise and stares at Solomon, then the screen. With her fingers, Laura twists and turns the 3D image as though she's searching for something.

"Lewis's family is downstairs in the basement, I'm sure of that. But I haven't been able to find any security cameras. Iris, are you able to locate any drones in the area?"

"None that I'm aware of. It seems the city or at least the building's surroundings are abandoned and silent."

"Any security cameras or tile cams?"

Jovan tries to focus though his mind is rushing with information overload. There are cameras in the tiles?

"Negative," Iris's voice booms around the white balcony. "This place is different from any of the other AR-cities I've been in."

"That's because it's not an AR-city," Solomon murmurs and keeps spinning the building, zooming it closer and then further back again. "Not an official one, anyway."

"It doesn't mean that the building doesn't need a security system," Luna says, waving her hand at Solomon to stop her fidgeting with the 3D building.

"Is that Novak?" Iris asks, surprise in her voice. "I thought she was sulking in her room because she got herself killed."

"Sorry to disappoint you," Luna says with an upbeat voice. "Not dead, not sulking."

"Whoop-dee-doo . . ." Iris's voice is just a whisper. Soon, Mrs. Salonen takes over.

"Luna, I am so incredibly delighted to hear your voice again. I know I owe you a visit, but things have been out of hand, to say the least. The war between United Inland and City of Finland is taking up all our time."

"Um, hi . . . " Luna hesitates. "Doctor Solomon's mother. I guess that'd be fine, you visiting me. The last time I saw you, you were in a stasis capsule downstairs from the resort's . . ."

"No time for a trip down memory lane," Solomon interrupts them with urgency in her voice. "Novak, what were you saying about the security cameras?"

Luna rolls her eyes. "Sorry, Solomon's mom. I guess we'll need to catch up some other time." Once she's by Laura's side, Luna reaches over and spins the 3D building, then zooms in further. At the doorway, a small screen with numbers appears. "Can we access that?"

Solomon taps the screen and enters a code. She swipes open a second keyboard for Luna, the kind the CS-keys used to have. "Here. Works just like the simple ones back home."

Luna's eyes narrow at the word simple, but after a moment's pause, she turns to focus on the keyboard and starts entering numbers. New windows pop open, but she doesn't stop for a second and just keeps on typing. Soon, a view of a room with a pool appears, then one with a fireplace. A staircase. A bedroom. Three hallways. An open-concept kitchen with no windows. Most of the rooms lack windows, Jovan suddenly realizes.

"See? A security system." Luna nods at the screen and takes a step back. "But where the hell are all the people?"

They study the feeds in focused silence.

"Wait, there's movement at the garden camera," Luna says and zooms in one of the screens. Silently, they all follow Luna's hovering finger, waiting by what looks like a dead vine tree. "There."

A blurred image of a woman wearing all black appears outside the building. With assured steps, she heads toward the keylock Luna used to hack into the building's security system.

"Margaret." Iris huffs. "Why is she out in the open? She's supposed to wait until we . . ." Iris grunts, lost in words. ". . . until we figure this fuckery out!"

"Can you contact her, sweetie?" Mrs. Salonen asks. Solomon's hand swipes, and a new window with a cursor opens. They all wait silently as Laura types and sends a message to Margaret's AR-glasses.

LEWIS. WE ARE NOT READY. BACK AWAY FROM THE TARGET.

On the screen, Margaret stops in the middle of the concrete yard. She raises her hand and puts the AR-glasses on her face, just to remove them again.

"What the hell is she doing?" Iris whispers. Jovan can hear her fingers tapping furiously at a keyboard. "Has she lost her hybrid mind?"

Solomon turns to stare at Luna. "Novak, you try talking to her. She won't talk to me but maybe she'll talk to you."

"It'll have to say the call's from me," Luna says to Solomon. "Not you."

Laura nods and types in a command. Soon, three dots appear on the egg's screen. In the feed, Margaret stops and reaches for the AR-glasses, but doesn't put them on.

Luna bites her lower lip and taps her foot. "Come on, come on, come on."

Finally, Margaret lifts the glasses to eye level. The buzzing must have annoyed her enough to do so. When she sees who's calling, she stops tapping on the keypad in front of her and puts on the glasses.

Luna clears her throat. "Margaret?"

"Hey. Luna."

"Hey, you. What are you doing out in the open? We're not ready to go in yet."

Luna can see what Margaret sees through the AR-glasses. It's close to what tapping used to feel like, but less intimate.

"I know. You're not. Ready. But I don't. Need. Your help. Luna." Margaret closes her eyes and tucks her chin. "Not this time."

"What do you mean? What's going on?"

Waiting for Margaret to answer her, Luna stares at what's in front of her. A yellow concrete wall with a keypad.

A woman's shoes, stained and orange.

"Marge, even if you know how to get in, we don't have any backup over there. Nurse Saarinen will take you down the second you walk in."

"She. Won't."

Luna frowns, feeling the gaze of everyone around her at the back of her neck. "What do you mean, she won't? Marge, have you been talking to Nurse Saarinen?"

Margaret doesn't reply, just fiddles with the keypad in front of her.

"You can't believe anything she tells you." Luna huffs, her eyes wide. "Marge, you know this! You're smarter than this!"

Blinking. A head shake. Then—a voice filled with pain and despair.

"She has. My family. Luna. She has. My *everything*."

Helpless and confused, Jovan watches Luna pace around the egg. Margaret had ended their call after her few words, then tapped her finger behind her right ear, turning off all sound from the outside world.

"We're going to lose her, Laura." Luna circles frantically, pulling her hair. "She doesn't care about anything anymore."

"Slow down, Novak." Solomon raises her hand, trying to stop Luna's pacing. Luna stops by the hand, turns around, and continues pacing in the other direction. "It's not like she said she's about to off herself. Did she, now?"

"It's not what she said. But how she said it."

"That makes no fucking sense . . . " Iris starts, but something stops her from ranting further. Probably Mrs. Salonen beside her.

"I wonder if she has a gun . . . " Solomon mumbles to herself, focusing on the screen where Margaret stands by the door, bent over the keypad. "I don't see her carrying a weapon."

Luna keeps shaking her head. "Now who's elementary?" Luna stops and stares at Solomon. She lets her hands fall to her sides. "Margaret doesn't need a gun. Not anymore."

Laura looks past the screens and straight at Luna. Her expression doesn't change. It's just as stern and static as ever. Iris swears in her native Icelandic. Mrs. Salonen exhales deeply. A sudden feeling of defeat fills the space. Jovan seems to be the only one who has no idea what's going on. Not until Luna's cracking voice states what all of them have come to understand.

"She's going to turn herself in. She's made a deal with Nurse Saarinen without us knowing about it." Luna looks up to the ceiling as to stop her tears. "Like that maniac would ever keep her word, whatever she's promised Margaret."

"She will," Laura says, her voice flat. "To make an example of her."

They watch Margaret move away from the door as it slowly slides open in front of her. She steps in, looks around, and then the door slides shut behind her.

Solomon starts tapping and swiping the screens. "The hallway camera. We should be able to follow her."

Luna's head jerks back. "*Follow* her? What are we going to do to *stop* her? Can't Bill send a missile or something? Can't we turn off the building? Hack Margaret's chip?"

Solomon frowns but doesn't interrupt her task to glance at Luna. "What missile? Bill doesn't have any weaponry. And I have no access to Nurse Saarinen's database, only the security system which is not integrated with her server."

"And her chip?"

Laura tilts her head, staring at Margaret. "It's still Lewis. I might get through her firewalls, but it'll take hours, if not days."

"There must be something we could do," Luna says, her eyes pleading. "You said Dennis has assets in the green city. That they're protected by his people. Can't they help?"

A hallway view opens on the hovering screen. Margaret walks around the room, opening doors and peeking her head in. She makes her way down the corridor.

Luna grunts and stomps the floor. "Fine. I'll ask Bill myself. And I'll be damned if I answer any of your questions from now on. We all know Bill despises you and would be glad to hear that I've taken over this ridiculous project egg or whatever the fuck . . ."

"It's not an army." Solomon sighs, her voice more flustered than usual. "Okay? Just one soldier. An asset. To keep them safe."

Luna cocks her head. "One soldier? That's it?"

"That's it."

"What good is one soldier going to do when Nurse Saarinen sends thousands of troops over to kill them all?"

"True, though it's not just any soldier."

Luna's eyes widen. She spreads her hands and raises her brows, gesturing for Laura to elaborate.

"It's Owena. Or the clone, that is."

Jovan can feel Luna's rushing mind, the way she's having more and more trouble controlling herself. "Owena's five years old and as odd as a headless duck!"

Solomon frowns but doesn't say anything. Mrs. Salonen clears her throat. "Is that some sort of a Serbian saying I haven't heard of? It's cute."

Luna spins around. "Do you know what your psycho daughter is talking about? Last I checked, Owena was a captive in City of Finland's Chip-Center with the other children you people stole while butchering the rest of us in Iceland."

Mrs. Salonen chuckles briefly. "Us people? I was there, remember? You released me. You and William."

Jovan has the hardest time keeping up. Luna's never told him what happened at the resort during what the Happiness-Program leaders call The Iceland Incident.

"And Owena? What the hell does Nurse Saarinen or any of this have to do with Owena?"

"There are two Owena's. The little girl from Kinship Care is with Nurse Saarinen, and this other one at the mansion is a clone. The clone was programmed to assassinate Dennis Jenkins, but he was able to reprogram the girl and make her an ally." Mrs. Salonen explains. "Both of the girls, Owena and her clone, are programmed with advanced combat skills. In some ways, the girl's now more machine than human."

"But how—"

"That has to wait," Solomon nods at the camera. In the current view, Margaret has made her way to the staircase with no door. A strange glow starts at the lower end of it, but the camera angle stops them from seeing what's downstairs. She starts down the stairs.

"Where's the basement camera?" Iris asks, tapping her keyboard. "I can't access it."

Laura doesn't reply but keeps working on the screens. After a moment of nothing happening, Luna stomps over and pushes Solomon aside. "Omnipotent, my ass . . . " she mumbles and enters a long snippet of code. Then she zooms the view wider and spins it up so they can all see.

The multicolored tiles are everywhere. Blues, greens, reds, purples, yellows, and oranges glimmer and blink around the basement with rows of stasis capsules attached to tubes and wires.

"Those don't look right," Iris says, wonder in her voice. "What is this place? When did you create a pod like that, Doctor Solomon?"

"I didn't."

"Did you?" Iris asks the woman in the same room with her.

"No, sweetie. I did not," Mrs. Salonen replies.

Luna kneels to breathe. She closes her eyes. The feeling of drowning begins again, and Jovan prepares for another trip to the unknown. But the sinking never starts. Luna opens her eyes, then tries again. She's tapping Margaret—to stop her from walking further into the basement—but the woman is not responding.

"Come on, Margaret," Luna whispers. Only Jovan can hear her pleading now. "We need you. I can't stop her without you. No one can."

At the farthest corner of the basement stand two stasis capsules, the steamed-up glass obscuring their contents. Between them, in the shadow of the pods, the silhouette of a woman is visible, waiting.

Margaret approaches, then stops before the figure hiding in the shadows. The two stand and stare at each other for the longest time.

"Is it buffering?" Iris asks, annoyance shading her voice. "Or is there no audio on this thing? What kind of tech has no sound?"

"Tech made of spare parts," Laura mumbles, her eyes never leaving the screen.

Luna moves closer to the doctor and lowers her voice. "If the shit hits the fan . . . Can you upload her?"

Solomon shakes her head once.

"Why not? You did it to me."

"That was different."

"Different how? Margaret's Unchipped too. Just, I don't know, a hybrid version."

"Her firewalls are unbreakable. Her chip is untraceable."

Jovan feels like screaming. None of this is good. None of this makes sense. Is Luna dead after all? Is this just some program based on her memories? Just behavioral data convincing him he hasn't lost the love of his life after all?

Is it just a stasis-induced dream?

"But you're a fucking *god*, Laura!" Luna insists. "Or an unstoppable force of, of . . . whatever!"

Solomon shrugs once. "It's Lewis. No one can access her firewalls and security system. Not without her permission."

"And that's why we need her to stay alive," Iris says. "How the hell are we going to stop this maniac otherwise? That's her in the shadow, isn't it? Nurse Saarinen?"

A nod. Solomon zooms in closer, but they still can't put a face on the silhouette.

Suddenly, the light on the stasis capsules fades out. Both the doors click open. Margaret rushes to the closer one and pulls the handle on the metal and glass door. Once it's open, she slips inside, at an angle where the camera can't see, and then pulls out a young woman, maybe a sixteen or seventeen-year-old.

"That's her daughter, right?" Iris asks, but no one answers.

Margaret helps the girl onto an operating table, carefully tucking her hair behind her ears. When Solomon zooms in, they see the girl's eyes are partly open, unfocused but not in stasis.

"Meredith. That's the girl's name. She's Unchipped," Mrs. Salonen explains, but Jovan's not sure to whom. "Nurse Saarinen's been using her to contact Margaret. The girl's mother, Mindy, is in the other capsule."

"In stasis?" Iris asks Mrs. Salonen.

"No, just heavily sedated."

Margaret hugs the girl against her chest. While they sway slowly, the silhouette finally steps out of the shadow. Nurse Saarinen walks over to what looks like a light switch and turns it on. An old-fashioned Faraday cage has been built between the stasis capsules. Inside, a desk and a gaming chair.

"That's why Margaret couldn't hack her chip," Mrs. Salonen says. "She's locked herself in a box."

Nurse Saarinen pulls out a wheelchair and pushes it over the second capsule. Once the girl is awake enough to sit without her mother's support, Margaret hurries to the wheelchair. Together, they pull a woman with a shaved head out of the capsule. Once Mindy sits in the wheelchair, Margaret strips off her coat and places it between Mindy's head and the back of the chair to stop her head from falling back.

One leg at a time, the girl makes her way down from the operating table. She walks over to her two moms. Margaret turns to smile at her, tears streaming down her cheeks. She strokes Meredith's face and pulls her in for another hug. When Nurse Saarinen says something none of them can hear, Margaret begins pushing the wheelchair toward the staircase.

"What the hell?" Iris murmurs. "She's letting them go?"

Meredith hurries to Margaret, pulling her arm to stop her. Gently Margaret takes the girl's hand

and hugs her, whispering something into her ear. Whatever she says, it makes Meredith cry harder.

Luna looks like she's crying, too, but no tears fall from her eyes. She cups her face with her palms and turns her back on the screen.

Solomon swipes the air and pulls a chair under her. She sits down and crosses her legs. "Two people are walking out of there today. But Lewis isn't one of them."

Laura swipes the air, and the view changes. Four women push the wheelchair to the stairs and then pull Mindy up. Slowly, they make their way up the multicolored stairs. Once they get to the corridor, Nurse Saarinen strides to the front door and types in a code.

"Can't we hack her chip now?" Iris asks no one in particular. "I know Lewis is a genius and all, but we aren't exactly half-wits ourselves. Mrs. Salonen and I have survived in the resort ruins for months and still have access to the outer world. You two are living inside a freaking supercomputer." She pauses to sigh. "There must be something we can do."

"Not in four minutes and thirty-seven seconds, we can't." Solomon peeks over her shoulder, but Luna doesn't meet her gaze. Pain has pushed her down onto the floor. She sits and waits quietly, hugging her legs against her chest.

Soon, the hallway camera shows two women, Margaret and Nurse Saarinen, returning without a wheelchair—and without Mindy and Meredith. They walk back toward the staircase, Nurse Saarinen's steps hurried. She disappears into the staircase's glow and doesn't bother to look back to see if Margaret is following her.

But she is.

The screens flicker from one to another until they're all looking at the basement again. The stasis capsules stand empty with their doors open. Nurse Saarinen is inside her cage between them, collecting an object from inside. While she prepares something with multiple wires and screws attached to it, Margaret walks to the operating table and leans back against it. Then she jumps up to sit on it and lies down. Eyes closed, she doesn't look around her. Doesn't say a word. Doesn't cry. She lies still, looking as if she's simply too exhausted to stay awake for what's to come.

"Is she drugged?" Iris asks.

Solomon briefly shakes her head no. "She's just done."

With brisk steps, Nurse Saarinen walks over to the operating table. She places a bulky helmet around Margaret's head and attaches a belt under her chin to keep the headwear from slipping off. Then she steps aside and sorts out the multiple wires, pulling them one by one to a machine at the end of the table.

"What kind of a mad scientist show is this?" Iris mumbles. Again, no one answers. Luna sobs silently on the floor, crying her tearless cry.

Nurse Saarinen pulls the enormous machine closer, pointing its beak at Margaret's head. A red laser light appears on the bulky helmet. Turning her back on the camera, Nurse Saarinen fires up a screen and an old-time computer.

"Do you know what that machine is, dear?" Mrs. Salonen asks Doctor Solomon.

"Mm," is all Laura replies.

"It's going to scan her brain, isn't it?"

"Not just scan," Solomon answers her mother. "It's going to slice it. That's the old way of mind mapping."

"It'll kill her." Iris's words are more a statement than a question for confirmation. "The very second the scan is done."

Jovan wishes he could turn off this feed. He wishes he could walk to Luna and wrap his arms around her, ease her agony. He wishes he wasn't stuck in this place. That Luna wasn't sort-of-dead. That Margaret wasn't tired of the fight. That she wouldn't give up on the burning world that so desperately needs her.

Oh, how he wishes—

The wave of light blinds him for several seconds. He tries to focus on the camera feed again, to see what happened to Margaret after the laser went off. But all he can hear is Luna's endless scream.

CHAPTER 3
DENNIS

The two of them—a young girl and a young woman—run around the avocado trees right outside the metal barn building. Their bare feet thump against the dead grass. Dennis sits in the shade, peeling an orange and watching the girls' never-ending game of tag.

It's been too long since the last time he's been home. Too long since he's felt the scorching sun against his tired face. Up here, the sunbeams always seem more merciless, like a mocking reminder of having to leave his beloved air-conditioned green city behind.

Not that his reunion with the mansion brings them safety. No, it's quite the opposite. Dennis's farm was the first place that Nurse Saarinen scanned when trying to find the rebel crew after they fled the green city. They had spread out and waited in the wilderness, until the last spy drone had buzzed away and back into the city. Who's to know when they'll come back around?

The war between the United Inland and City of Finland. That's the only thing buying them some time, as Nurse Saarinen and her troops are solely focused on killing off the resistance back at the East-Land. Until the nurse vanquishes the black market and CFU, her resources—including the deadly missiles—are limited and solely to be used for this purpose. Dennis and the crew William now leads may have become Nurse Saarinen's afterthought, but there's no doubt in Dennis's mind that she wouldn't spare a few drones or a small army with weaponry, if one of the escapees was spotted roaming outside the mansion.

"Watch out for black widows, Sanna!" he yells, his mouth full of sweet fruit. "And stay under the roof, okay?"

The younger girl, Sanna, has bent over an old ladder by the furthest horse stall, investigating its rotting surface. But Sanna can't hear him. Bulky, noise-canceling headphones cover her ears—protection against the Chipped's sonic weapon that is deadly to any Unchipped individual. Sanna wears the headphones each time they visit the barn to get some fresh air.

But she's not the younger one, Dennis reminds himself for what must be the hundredth time. It seems impossible for him to remember, no matter how many days go by. *Sanna's twice as old as Owena is.*

Despite the raggedy homemade helmet that looks like a cage for some sort of a rodent, Owena moves around like a puma, her thirty-something-year-old body perfectly aligned with her five-year-old mind. The hat is to protect her from another kind of a weapon—chip hacking.

This clone Nurse Saarinen made is deadly in the wrong hands, but ever since Dennis pulled her out of the Chip-Center's glass prison, the girl's been nothing but a fun-loving, ice-cream-craving, in nearly all ways normal five- or six-year-old kid. Just as Sanna needs the headphones, Owena has to wear the protective cage-hat whenever she's outside. Maria and Bill have built an intricate network of the wires and scraps in each room of the mansion to produce the same effect indoors, so any Chipped people inside should be safe from chip hacking.

A real person. That's what Owena is, and Dennis has come to care about the girl a great deal. Only her uncanny ability to move about like a ninja and never to miss the bullseye with a crossbow or even a nerf gun tells those around her that she's not just an ordinary girl. That, and the fact that she looks like an adult.

Dennis crosses his arms on his chest and closes his eyes. Yes, it's good to be home. Things haven't gone their way since he lost his role as the head of the Happiness-Program, but at least he has this. Home. The mansion. Even the raw, painful memories of losing his family don't affect him the way he first thought they would. Because he has something real now.

Allies.

Friends.

A new kind of family.

Distracted by his thoughts, Dennis bemusedly watches Owena knocking two rocks together. It's not until he sees the first sparks that Dennis jumps up and hurries to the girl. After kneeling down next to Owena, Dennis puts his hand gently on hers and smiles. "Why don't we find some other toy to play with, hon?" Carefully, he removes the rocks from Owena's hands. He straightens the cage-hat on her head and gives her an encouraging smile to let her know she's not in trouble.

Sanna follows them closely, her head tilted and face full of wonder. She pushes the headphones back. "But Mister Jenkins, why are you stopping her? She's teaching me survival skills. You know, so when the bad guys come and kill all the grown-ups, we'll still know how to cook for ourselves. And you can't cook without fire."

Dennis turns slightly so he can see Sanna's face better. "Now, where is this coming from, Sanna? All the grown-ups dying?"

The girl pouts and looks down at her toes. "They already killed the best one."

Lewis. Of course.

"Hey, maybe she's with your mother," Dennis suggests but instantly regrets his words. Creating false hope is not going to help Sanna in the long run, and the girl hates it when people call Doctor Solomon her mother. "Sorry, hon. I mean maybe Margaret's now with Doctor Solomon."

"Doctor Solomon says that she's not in the egg," Sanna says, poking the ground with her big toe. "And it's okay if you want to call her my mother. I know it's true and all. I just don't want to."

"And why is that, hon?" Dennis asks out of pure curiosity.

"Because she's always telling me that family should stick together. And she's in that scary place, and I'm down here with you and Markus and the others, and I don't want things to change again."

"What does that have to do with calling her your mother?"

An angry frown shadows Sanna's face. "If I decide that you are my family, not her, then I'm doing as I'm told. I'm sticking together with my family."

Dennis exhales and nods slowly. "I see."

The sad pout returns to Sanna's face. "And now Margaret is dead. And maybe soon, all of you will be too. But I'm not going to go to that scary egg place. I'm staying here. And that's why Owena needs to teach me how to make a fire. It's one of the things Nurse Saarinen taught her."

Owena nods and reaches for the rocks in Dennis's hands. Puzzled and out of words, he lets the girl take them. "Okay, but if you want to make a fire, we need a safe place to do that."

"Okay . . . " Sanna says and frowns. "Like what?"

"Like a metal bucket or a fire pit. I'll find something from the garage later. Why don't you two play something else for now?" He hopes they'll simply forget the fire-making game and focus on something less destructive.

As the girls shrug and run down the barn aisle to the jump rope that's attached to the metal stall door, Dennis sinks back into his thoughts.

Lewis was never exactly his favorite person, not even back when they were all just founders in a promising Finnish pharmaceutical company. When she sold Doctor Solomon out and started working with the rebels, Dennis had despised Margaret. Called her a traitor. A fraud. But now he understands. He gets why the Unchipped are important and why the utopia the Happiness-Program allegedly brings might be everything but. He gets Lewis now. Now, when it's too darn little, too darn late.

Two sparks fly through the air, landing in a tuft of dead grass. The headphones fall off her head as Sanna jumps in place, clapping her hands together excitedly. The pout is just a memory as she stares at the small flames licking the dry grass just outside the metal building.

Dennis gets up in a hurry and runs to the small fire by the jumping rope. He stomps on the tiny flames, out of breath and baffled. Then he turns and picks the headphones off the ground, placing them back on Sanna's head. He had forgotten how all-consuming looking after young children can be.

"Okay, little ladies." Once the fire is safely put out, Dennis turns to Owena and gestures for her to hand over the rocks. "Let's not burn down the whole farm, shall we?"

Her beautiful face twitches twice. A side-effect from the cloning, maybe?

"What's a farm?" Owena asks, her head tilted to the side. Sometimes, she moves like a ninja, sometimes more like a robot.

Dennis tosses the rocks into the bushes. He extends one hand to Owena, then the other hand to Sanna.

"How about I explain that to you over a nice, thick stack of pancakes? What do you say?"

The short journey from the barn back to the mansion always makes him nervous. Dennis had insisted that Bill give the girls thirty minutes of playtime outside under the barn's protective roof each day. They are both too young to learn what cabin fever feels like, spy drones or no spy drones hovering nearby. If Nurse Saarinen's spyware were to locate a Chipped rebel, she could hack and fry their chips in a matter of seconds. And now that Lewis is gone, their firewalls are hopelessly expired. Dennis is sure Iris and Luna are more than capable when it comes to programming, but they're still a far cry from Margaret's genius-level coding skills. Even Doctor Solomon has confirmed that when it comes to firewalls, Lewis was one of a kind.

"Stay away from drones, and you'll be okay," Iris had told Dennis the other day. "Your firewalls should protect you from any long-distance hacking."

"But they won't protect us from drones?" Dennis had asked. "Why is that?"

"Because if a drone locates and identifies a fugitive," Iris had explained, "it's not so much a hacking anymore, but Nurse Saarinen's personal chip barbeque. They'll literally fry your brain."

Hand in hand, they walk toward the mansion. Dennis looks up and sees Bill and Maria standing on the front porch. Bill fills one bird feeder after another, while Maria grips her sniper rifle and stares straight at them, her foot tapping.

"Are we late, Mister Jenkins?" Sanna asks when she sees Maria's serious face.

"Just a tad, sweetheart. Just a tad."

But Sanna can't hear him. "Is she angry?" she half-whispers. "She looks angry."

Owena lets go of Dennis's hand and hurries to walk next to Sanna. She reaches for her headphones and lifts one of the earmuffs gently. "I can tackle her. Do you want me to?" Owena asks, "So we can run upstairs and lock ourselves in our room?"

Dennis stops walking and stutters while trying to find the right words. "That . . . we don't do that, Owena. Not to Maria. She's our friend. Our ally. You remember what that is, right? An ally?"

Owena stares at him for a few seconds, then nods. They continue to the porch, where Dennis lets go of the girls' hands and lets them run inside.

"See any drones, doll?" he asks Maria once he steps up onto the porch. Calling her a doll is an inside joke, though the woman hardly laughs at her nickname. But her tolerating Dennis's attempts at humor is more than progress when it comes to the two of them. He still fantasizes about her, of course. But since Dennis has been in charge of the girls' safety, his obsession with Maria has mellowed out.

"Do you see me shooting metal birds out of the sky?" Maria asks listlessly. The tiniest smile twitches her lips when she turns her gaze from the clouds to Dennis. "I see you still have a death wish."

"Why's that?"

"For calling me doll."

Dennis grins at the woman and heads toward the front door.

"You're late." Bill's words stop Dennis in his tracks. Though his voice is filled with disapproval, Bill never turns his focus from the bird feeders to look at Dennis.

"Sorry, boss," Dennis says lightly. "Won't happen again."

His words make Bill's hands freeze on the feeder. The sugary liquid drips from the small pouch as he looks at Dennis, an astonished look on his face.

"Why so surprised, son? You think I have a problem with the tables turning?" Dennis chuckles briefly and points at Bill. "You're the captain now." Then he points at his own chest. "Me? I'm just here to put out small fires and cook pancakes for my girls."

Forks clink against the plates as Dennis's new family—Bill, Maria, Micky, Kaarina, Yeti, Markus, Sanna, and Owena—finishes the banana walnut pancakes. It's too late for breakfast, but the groceries are running dangerously low. All that's left is breakfast stuff, so they've had that for lunch—and dinner—for several days.

Micky and Maria are having a hard time locating anyone selling black-market goods ever since Nurse Saarinen has had the black market on the run. Anyone without a functioning chip was already cautious about strangers, but now that Nurse Saarinen is telling people to hunt them down, all communication among survivors outside the city has ceased. Jenny's still out there, so is the CFU. But they haven't heard from their allies about the next food delivery.

"Can I have some milk, please?"

Markus looks up at Owena, his mouth filled with pancake. He gestures at the pantry in the front hallway. "Go geb somph."

"Milk powder's almost gone," Yeti says, his voice low. "Plenty of water left, though."

Maria and Kaarina look up from their plates, then at each other, then focus on the pancakes again, not bothering to comment on the milk situation.

Markus chews slowly and stares at Yeti. "Just let them have some milk. What's the big deal?"

"I don't know about you," Yeti says, stacking his fork full of pancake, "But I'd rather not starve to death while we figure out a new source for supplies."

"We got plenty left. And Jenny will be back any day now," Markus says, pointing his fork at Yeti. "Besides, without a certain gourmand, maybe we wouldn't have to worry about this potential issue in the first place."

Yeti grunts and waves Markus off.

"All of y'all's fine-dining asses are getting the exact same amount of chow," Bill chimes in. "That's the deal. Micky decides what we eat and when we eat. Right, Micky?"

For a moment, Micky stops chewing and side-eyes Bill. Then he glances at Yeti. Micky clears his throat and lifts a finger, gesturing that he'll need time to finish his bite. Chewing slowly, looking up toward the ceiling, his finger still pointing up, Micky buys his time.

"Oh, for fuck's sake." Yeti grunts and tosses his fork on the empty plate. The loud clinking sound makes Sanna jump on her seat. Yeti waves Owena off toward the pantry. "Just go get the damn milk, kid."

"And bring us some cheesecake from the fridge, too, while you're at it," Bill calls after her.

Yeti looks at Bill in disbelief. "We're having a party now too? Open house? Food for everyone?"

"Honey, don't sweat . . . "

"Who the fuck made cheesecake?"

"Now, now," Dennis says to Bill and Yeti, his voice calm. "Jenny will be back from the city any day now. The CFU has never come up empty-handed. I'm sure we'll have plenty of food then."

Owena stands by the table, staring at the men. Her head turns toward whoever's talking at the moment like she's watching a game of ping-pong. When Dennis smiles at her and nods at the pantry, she adjusts the cage-hat on her head and stomps off.

"I thought she didn't need that thing inside the house?" Kaarina half-whispers, looking at Bill. "It's not like we didn't install a mountain of that metal stuff on the walls."

Bill shrugs and wets his lips. "We did."

"So why is she wobbling around with it like a drunken mouse in a trap?" Maria asks.

Another shrug. "I guess she likes it."

Markus pushes his plate forward on the table and leans on his elbows. He looks around at everyone at the table. "Maybe we should all wear something similar."

"All of us?" Yeti grunts. "Last I checked you and Mister Moneybags here were the only Chipped people living in this house. You and the mouse-trap girl."

"Okay, so Faraday cage for me and Dennis." Markus nods. "And headphones for you guys. I mean, who knows how long it'll take for her to locate us? She has unlimited resources now."

"Who?" Sanna asks, her eyes wide. "Doctor Solomon?"

"No, Nurse Saarinen, you ding-dong, not your mother," Yeti says but gives Sanna a conciliatory smile. As soon as Yeti realized the mistake he's made, he makes a face. "Shit! Sorry, kid. I mean Doctor Solomon."

Sanna narrows her eyes at Yeti and sticks out her tongue. Yeti chuckles at her and then sticks out his tongue as well.

Owena sits down next to Sanna. After a long gulp of milk, she looks up and burps. Nobody reacts.

"What's a gourmand?" she asks.

At the exact same time, Markus, Maria, and Micky point their forks at Yeti. The big man rolls his eyes at their grinning faces, gets up, and takes his dishes to the sink. He washes his plate, murmuring something in his native Finnish.

"Markus does have a point," Dennis says when everyone seems to be finished with their pancakes. "Now that Lewis is gone—"

"Her name is Margaret," Sanna corrects Dennis.

"Sorry, sweetie. Now that we don't have Margaret to protect us, we should really take precautions. And not just us Chipped people. According to Doctor Solomon, it sounds like Nurse Saarinen is making progress figuring out the Unchipped wiring issue, or whatever it is, as well."

"Speaking of which," Kaarina says. "When is our dear doctor going to share some of this news with us? I know Bill's been asking to meet with her, but something always comes up. Something's not right here. I mean, Doctor Solomon started this whole thing. She should be calling us, not the other way around. We never planned to stay up here for this long. We should be on our way to a safe place by now, and Solomon's the only one who can arrange that. But we have barely heard from her. What's up with that?"

"It's true," Dennis says. "It's very unlike Laura to be like this."

"I mean." Kaarina huffs. "She *knows* that Sanna's safety depends on this!"

Bill groans and adjusts the rubber band around his dreadlocks. "One thing's for sure . . . This waiting shit sucks. One noise from outside in the middle of the night and I soil my pajama bottoms, thinking that Nurse Saarinen has finally sent out a missile to take us down. I mean, I guess Solomon's occupied dealing with the war in United Inland and having to save Margaret's family and all, but while we wait to figure what the hell is going on in our brains, sure as shit Nurse Saarinen's crew is researching and probing away in their evil underground labs."

"Then *someone* should push for an emergency meeting with Laura. We'll have to make our move sooner than later. As long as we just stay here in the mansion, we're just a row of sitting ducks," Maria says.

They all stare at Bill, who's digging into the dish of cheesecake Owena brought him. While they wait, he cuts himself a big piece of cake and takes more than a bite. As the silence around him continues, he looks up and raises his eyebrows. "Whab?"

"The chip issue?" Maria says.

"Doctor Solomon?" Kaarina continues.

"An emergency meeting?" Markus suggests.

Bill nods rapidly. After swallowing a big chunk of cake, he says, "Totally agree. Someone should make this happen, and preferably yesterday. Shit's urgent. This is our brains we're talking about."

Dennis clears his throat. "Son. I think your friends are trying to say that it should be the rebel leader who makes this emergency meeting happen."

Bill puts down the spoon and grabs a handful of cake. Licking the whipped cream off his fingers, he focuses on chewing the treat while nodding at Dennis's words. "Mm-hm, yup! Most def."

Kaarina sighs and buries her face in her palms.

Maria tilts her head and grins. "That's you, Bill. Our mighty, fearless, dairy-defying leader."

"Oh shit." Bill wipes his hands together and grins back at Maria. "That is me!" He pushes the cheesecake toward Micky and gets up. "I'm on it, just need the encrypted AR-glasses from upstairs." He takes off toward the spiral staircase.

The two young girls get up as well and follow Bill upstairs.

The rest of them sit in silence, all lost in their thoughts. It's getting dark outside. Dennis can hear a coyote call for its pack through the open kitchen window, but no one else seems to notice the sound.

Maria's the first to break the silence. "Here's the thing. I get your point, Markus," Maria nods at the Chipped man with overgrown hair, "but even if we do get away from here, are we all supposed to wear a cage over our heads or walk around with noise-canceling headphones for the rest of our lives? I mean, Margaret being a genius aside, she had a plan and a vision for a long-term solution."

Kaarina looks up from her hands. "Right. Dechipping."

Maria pauses to see everyone's reactions. Markus adjusts his seat. Micky presses down on the small crumbs of cake on the table and licks them off his fingers. Dennis gives Maria a smile, gesturing for her to continue.

"I say we keep going." She pauses, but no one says anything. "With the dechipping. We don't need Margaret to execute the plan. We need a surgeon and a safe place where Nurse Saarinen can't get to us. And we have one of two."

"I'll ask Jenny to talk to Dr. Baldwin," Dennis says. "The CFU might be able to smuggle him out of the city. Just like they helped us escape. Maybe he'll be able to bring the mobile surgery center with him."

Markus opens his mouth, then decides against speaking.

Kaarina bites her lower lip. "I agree with Maria. Let's get this chip junk out of our heads That's the only way to be safe from the frequency attacks and the brain hacking."

Markus leans forward over the table. "And this Baldwin doctor. Is he trustworthy?"

"He is," Dennis says. "I'll give you my word."

"Baldwin's the one who fixed my wiring," Maria says, "after I was used as the Chipped's personal killer robot."

Dennis looks at Maria apologetically. She lifts her hand. "Let's just focus on the task at hand. All in favor of dechipping, as soon as Baldwin arrives at the mansion?"

"Hey, should we wait for Bill and Yeti before voting?" Dennis says, hesitating to call Yeti by his nickname. No one seems to know his real name, and Dennis has never thought of asking why.

Micky waves his hand. "No bother, *chicos*. No one wants that *mierda* out of their heads as badly as Beau does."

Everyone but Markus turns to look at Kaarina. Before speaking, she gives an apologetic look to Markus. Why, Dennis is not sure. Kaarina gestures at the ceiling, toward where Yeti's room is located. "He never wanted to be Chipped in the first place. He won't talk about it, but he once mentioned to Luna that the same thing happened to him that happened to her. They did the chipping against his will."

"Christ," Dennis says, inhaling sharply. "But that's against the protocol."

"A lot of what happened in the cities was anything but protocol." Markus rubs his neck and finally throws his hands in the air. "I'm in. I'm tired of waiting for us to win this war. I guess for all this time, I've figured that the Happiness-Program itself isn't a bad thing, but for the people running it. But I guess there'll always be some new maniac to take over, even if we conquer the one who's in charge now."

Maria looks at Kaarina, who raises her eyebrows at her. "Do you really need to ask?"

Maria looks at Micky, who flicks his fingers next to his temple, gesturing that he's ready to get rid of what's inside.

Maria looks at Dennis. Those mesmerizing eyes still make him wonder how he ever lived without such an angelic creature by his side. Or if not by his side, at close proximity anyway. *For you, doll, anything,* he thinks. *For you, I'd cut off my whole head.*

"Dennis?"

He clears his throat and blushes. "Yes, Maria. I support this plan."

Maria leans back in her chair. A satisfied smile lingers on her face. She reaches for her empty water glass and raises it. "To dechipping. And to fearless, genius Margaret. Our hero who started this mad plan in the first place."

Dennis listens to Bill's bare feet flap against the balcony's tiles as he paces around with AR-glasses on his face. Maria, Kaarina, Markus, and Yeti lean against the balcony's railing, eyes lazily following Bill as he gestures and rants.

Alone, Dennis sits inside, right next to the open balcony doors. The gaming chair feels comforting under his weight. The chair doesn't struggle and groan when he sits like it did before. Being away from the city has been good for his health—mental *and* physical. He stares at the distant green glow that used to be his home, a safe haven. Now, it belongs to his worst enemy. The only thing that City of California gives Dennis today is a constant fear of spy drones. Drones equipped with deadly sonic weapons and cameras, sent out to locate him and his newfound family.

"No, Laura. No." Bill pulls on his dreads and stops right in front of Kaarina, seemingly staring straight at her. But through the glasses, he's somewhere with Doctor Solomon, negotiating a long overdue deal. "No, we've had it with this fuckery. Either you tell us what's up with our—No! If we suggest that to her, she'll never trust us again. I'm telling you . . . no, no! Listen—" Bill closes his eyes, clearly frustrated by one too many interruptions. He stops and fills his lungs with air, then groans loudly in frustration. "Christ on a pole. For the last time, Laura . . . No."

A careful knock on the door distracts Dennis. He swings the gaming chair around and stares at Sanna's pouting face in the door. "What's going on, sweetheart?"

"I'm hungry."

"Okay . . ." Dennis takes a quick look at Bill and his allies on the balcony. "I'm sure Micky can help you fix a late-night snack."

"Micky's reading us a bedtime story. Owena likes it, but I don't."

"What's the story called?"

"*The Shining*."

Dennis remembers the classics by heart. Someone must have found the book in the master bedroom. Micky and Bill live in that room. There are not enough CCs in this world to make Dennis set foot in there ever again.

"Can you come with me?" Sanna asks, blinking her long eyelashes. "Downstairs to the pantry?"

Dennis gets up and walks to the doorway, kneeling to be on the same level with the girl. "It's okay. Go and pick out anything you want, sweetie. If someone sees you, just tell them that I asked you to bring me a snack. Okay?"

She looks down at the floor, a worried look on her face.

"I'm telling you, sweetheart. I'll protect you from the big bad Yeti. Just go eat."

"It's not that."

"What is it, then?"

"I'm afraid."

"Afraid of what?"

"To go downstairs alone. At first I wasn't, but now I am. It's a stupid story, but a scary story."

The book. Of course. Why in the world has Micky picked a horror story to read to a five- and ten-year-old? Doesn't he know anything about kids?

Just as Dennis gets up and extends his hand for Sanna to grab, Maria clears her throat behind them. Holding hands, Dennis and Sanna turn around to stare at her. Sanna smiles at Maria. "Mister Jenkins is hungry. He needs a snack, so I'm helping him get one."

"I see." An unsure smile lingers on Maria's face. "Well, Mister Jenkins is more than welcome to go to the pantry. It's his house, after all. And it's not him that I need. It's you."

Sanna blinks rapidly, staring at Maria. "Me?"

Maria looks back at Bill with pleading eyes. Bill lowers his gaze and shakes his head.

"Yes, you. We have a favor to ask."

Sanna lets go of Dennis's hand, looking up at him, then back at Maria. "What kind of favor?"

Gently, Dennis places his hand protectively on Sanna's shoulder. "I don't think Sanna's the right person to help us with this problem," he says, and frowns. The desperation lingers around them, making Dennis wary and slightly nervous. It's clear to him that Maria isn't happy about whatever it is they're about to suggest to Sanna. In fact, none of them seem happy about it.

Maria nods at the balcony and smiles at Sanna. "Just come hear us out. Then you can decide if you want to help or not. Totally up to you."

Sanna takes a few steps toward the balcony and stops. She turns, extending her hand. Dennis takes it and follows her toward the green glow.

Outside on the balcony, Markus holds the AR-glasses in his hands. Bill, Kaarina, and Yeti whisper to one another in the further corner. Bill tosses his hands dramatically in the air whenever Kaarina or Yeti says anything. "But what choice do we have?" Bill snarls.

Markus sits on the tiles and leans against the railing, patting the spot next to him. "Come sit, Sanna. Let's have a small chat."

Sanna hurries to Markus and sits right next to him. The girl's always trusted the Finnish Chipped man more than anyone else in the group. The bond between them is undeniable.

Dennis returns inside and sits back in the gaming chair. He should be able to hear the conversation from here. And from this odd group, Markus is the only one who seems to have some kind of an understanding when it comes to communicating and dealing with children.

Markus turns a bit to get a better look at Sanna. He lifts the AR-glasses in his hand. "Guess who I've got on the line?"

Sanna's whole face brightens up in a matter of seconds. "I knew it was just another trick. I knew she wasn't dead for real!"

Concern visits Markus's face. "We've been through this, Sanna. You know your moth … " Markus stops and clears his throat. "You know Doctor Solomon is not dead … Oh."

Disappointment spreads on Sanna's face. Lewis. That's who she thought was calling.

"Hey, I really liked her too," Markus says, bumping his shoulder gently against Sanna's. "We all did. Margaret was one of the good ones."

"The best."

Markus nods at Sanna's words. "By far. And in a way, she's still with us. Her plan is going to help us start over somewhere where Owena doesn't need to wear that silly hat, and you won't need to wear headphones every time you go outside."

"I don't mind wearing them. And I like Owena's hat. It's funny."

Markus gives the girl a sad smile. "I like the way you think. And you're very brave."

"You could be brave too."

Markus laughs briefly, narrowing his eyes at Sanna. "Who says I'm not?"

Sanna's eyes flicker to Kaarina, standing further away with Yeti, Maria, and Bill. With a small sigh, she leans closer to Markus and whispers something in his ear. The man clears his throat, his cheeks slightly flushed. "It's complicated."

"No, it's not," Sanna says, a confident look on her face. "You just need to tell her."

Dennis leans closer in the gaming chair. Does Markus have a thing for Kaarina? Of course. That explains the ongoing bickering between the two Finnish men. It's no secret to anyone that Kaarina sneaks into Yeti's room every single night, or vice versa.

"Listen," Markus says, shaking his head. "About that favor. You're not going to like it and I hate to ask. And I wouldn't even bring this up if it wasn't the only option we have. We'd like to send you on a . . ." Flustered Markus looks up at his allies, then sighs and looks at Sanna again. "It's kind of like an adventure."

"An adventure outside the wired fence? Down the stream?"

Markus shakes his head no. "No, this is a whole new kind of place. Somewhere not many people have been. Someplace only very special, intelligent people get to go."

Sanna pauses to think. "Did Margaret go to this place?"

Markus thinks awhile, then starts nodding. "As a matter of fact, she did. Yes."

"Well, where is this place?"

"It's somewhere high. Up in the clouds. It's where your . . ." Markus stops to think. "It's where Doctor Solomon lives."

Sanna's eyes widen in horror. "At the egg place?" She slides a bit further away from Markus. Like she's looking for a way out, Sanna glances over at Dennis. He lifts his hand, gesturing for Sanna to stay put.

It's okay, kid. You can just say no, Dennis thinks, wishing he was Unchipped so the girl could hear his silent encouragement.

"Please don't make me go to the egg place, Markus." Sanna's pleading is loud. It stops the fierce conversation on the corner of the balcony. "Please, I'll do anything else. I won't eat anything tomorrow. I won't eat anything ever again. Just don't make me go to the egg place."

Kaarina rushes over and kneels next to Markus. "Sanna, hey." She reaches for Sanna's hand, but the girl shies away from Kaarina's touch. Dennis can't remember the girl ever doing anything like that before. "It's okay. It's just a visit, not a permanent thing."

Her black hair falls on her face as Sanna hugs her legs and lowers her chin.

"Your . . . Doctor Solomon just wants to see you. She misses you."

"Don't call her that," Sanna murmurs, her face buried between her arms.

"I didn't call her anything," Kaarina hurries to say, "I know how you feel about calling her anything but—"

"She is not my real mother!"

Markus looks at Kaarina and gestures for her to back off. When he moves closer to Sanna, the girl doesn't move away. "No one's going to make you go if you don't want to. Okay?" Markus pauses when Sanna fidgets away from him again, closer to the balcony door and Dennis. "But I had to ask. We'll find some other way, don't worry."

Bill and the others are getting restless. Mixed feelings visit their faces as they stare at Sanna in desperation.

"That's just kick-in-the-face . . . motherfucking . . . great," Bill mumbles and kicks something on the balcony tiles.

"Hey, take it easy," Markus snaps at Bill. "If Sanna's not up for it, then she's not up for it."

Sanna has started to cry. Dennis huffs, contemplating whether to jump up and interrupt this so-called negotiation gone terribly wrong.

Bill moves over to talk to Sanna. "Your moth . . . I mean, what's her face . . . *Doctor Solomon* has some information that we need."

Bill has kneeled but hasn't come too close to Sanna. If one more person touches the girl, she'll storm away from the balcony, Dennis is sure. Bill is smart. He knows this.

"It sucks rocks, Sanna, just to ask this from you. But without that information, we don't know if Margaret's plan is safe or not."

The Unchipped question. That's what they're after. What makes an Unchipped brain an Unchipped brain? If anyone can figure it out, it'll be Nurse Saarinen . . . or the ghost of Sanna's uploaded mother. Even Baldwin wouldn't know what happens to an Unchipped person if the chip is removed. No one's ever done it.

"Hey, it's like ripping off a bandage," Bill says. "You'll be back before you know it, eating double-layered cheesecake with me and Micky."

Bill hasn't touched Sanna, but extending his hand to move her hair behind her ear is enough to send the girl up from the balcony floor and back inside to where Dennis is sitting.

"You can't make me," she yells to Bill. "You're not my real mother, either."

Dennis opens his mouth to ask Sanna to stop but decides to stay put and watch her storm out instead. No promise of cheesecake, adventure, or any other treat can hold her back. The bedroom door slams behind him.

"Well, that went fucking well," Maria says, spreading her arms. She turns and leans against the railing, letting her upper body and head hang over.

"If Solomon doesn't get to see that kid, we'll never be ready for the dechipping." Kaarina sits down next to Markus on the tiles. She exhales in frustration while Markus closes his eyes and doesn't say a word.

"What if we blackmail Solomon instead?" Yeti asks. "What if we tell her that we'll hurt her daughter if she doesn't agree to help us?"

They all look at each other with wide eyes, then turn to stare at Yeti in horror.

"What?" the big man asks, crossing his arms. "*Obviously* it's a lie. I would never hurt Sanna, not in a million years. We just need to make Solomon believe that Sanna's in danger."

"Of all your caveman, shit-for-brains ideas, this takes the cake," Bill snaps at Yeti, "Do you really think that Solomon would ever fall for that? Huh? The most intelligent fucking," Bill twirls his hand in the air, trying to find the right word, "*being* or *thing* or whatever the fuck she is. Solomon *knows* we fucking love that kid!"

"What then?" Yeti growls at Bill. "Please, enlighten me. Because your cheesecake bribery was just as ridiculous as Markus promising the kid a goddamn *adventure*. I mean, I wouldn't set a foot in that freaking hellhole if you paid me."

"Well, good thing it's not your pretty-boy face Solomon's asked to see, either!" Bill's voice is so high it's squeaking.

"Okay, are you two boneheads done with your little pissing contest?" Maria steps between the two men, raising her hands. "You can continue acting like two bitches in heat once we've figured out what the hell we're going to say to Solomon."

Markus kicks the AR-glasses on the floor, sliding them toward Maria. "She's still there. Waiting. You tell her that her own daughter refuses to see her. Because . . . *not it!*"

Maria grunts in frustration but doesn't say anything back. She kicks the AR-glasses and heads back toward the corner. The glasses slide across the open balcony doorway, all the way to Dennis. He lifts his shoe and carefully stops the glasses with his foot.

Staring at the familiar gadget, an idea enters his mind. A genius idea.

Dennis reaches for the glasses and gets up. The gaming chair spins around its axle, suddenly lacking his body weight. Slow steps take him onto the balcony. No one looks up. All desperate and flustered, Dennis's allies are lost in their own thoughts.

"Well, gals and gents. Maybe there is another way."

A few grunts and shrugs. That's all he gets. The only person who perks up is Maria. And even her expression is skeptical at best.

"I may not be a genius with coding or medical skills. I'm not even a leader of anything anymore. All I have is this mansion, the limo parked in the garage, and a bank account full of CCs that I can't use."

"We know all this, Texas," Bill says, his tone warm but hopeless. "What's your point?"

He taps the AR-glasses against his palm, staring at their scratched surface. One of the earpieces is secured with duct tape. "Like I said, I'm no genius—but I am the best negotiator in City of California. And the first rule of negotiating is to never accept the conditions first handed to you. If you don't like the lawyer working for you, hire another one."

Maria crosses her arms, staring at Dennis with new interest. "Lawyer? You mean Laura." Her brow furrows more. "What makes you think you of all people can force Solomon to spill the beans? Without us delivering Sanna to her?"

Dennis smiles at her, pointing the glasses at Maria. "I can't make Laura Solomon do anything she doesn't want to. No one can." Dennis smiles and walks to Maria. He grabs hold of her hands and places the AR-glasses on her palms, closing her fingers around them. "But Solomon's not the only ally you have up *there*."

CHAPTER 4
MARIA

"But why is it all white?" Maria takes an uncertain step forward in the glow, keeping her eyes on the woman in a lab coat in the distance. The grinning Luna beside her doesn't reply. "I thought you said she can create any kind of scenery?"

Luna leans closer to half-whisper in Maria's ear. "She can. And she did."

"So, it's a . . ." Maria walks a semi-circle and turns to face Luna again. "It's an egg?"

"Not exactly. That's just what we call it. I think she just wants to have a clean space with zero interruptions."

"Can she hear us? Is she even here?"

"Yes, she's here. But I'm not sure if she's listening in. I'm not sure what her meeting with Bill was about, but she was in a dick mood when she came to tell me I have a visitor."

Maria takes a long look at the white lab coat at the back end of this strange space. It's strange how she despises Solomon, but at the same time, she feels sorry about the woman's daughter not wanting to see her.

"It was supposed to be Sanna visiting Laura," Maria says, lowering her voice to a whisper. "Not me visiting you."

"Why didn't Sanna come?"

"She's scared shitless of this place." Maria stops talking before saying the other reason why Sanna's not here right now. "It's not just the egg that bothers her. She's unsure of how she feels about her mother. Unsure enough to not even call her mom."

"Oh."

"Yeah." Maria gives Luna a quick, sad smile. "Oh is right."

"I think it's best we give her some space," Luna says, and grabs Maria's hand. Maria lets Luna walks her toward a door that seems to appear out of nowhere. Ever since the rebel crew found each other, most of them opted to keep their connection open at all times. The tapping and the fact that they practically lived inside each other's heads has made them close. Though Maria's never spent time in Luna's physical presence, she feels like they've known each other for a small eternity.

"And what's behind this door? More depressing, clinical white nothingness?"

"Pff. Not even close." Luna lets go of Maria's hand and swipes the air. The door swooshes open, revealing a cozy yellow room with at least six dogs lying around on the floor and a mattress in the middle of the space. Luna walks in and kneels on the floor. She whistles twice, and the dogs trot over to her and Maria. Luna scratches one of them behind the ears, laughing happily. "This is my room. No doom and gloom here. But plenty of dogs."

Maria looks down and lets her knuckles brush against the digital dog greeting her. "But they're not real. Right? None of this is."

Luna gets up and walks over to the mattress. When she sits down, she exhales and shakes her head at Maria. "Feels real to me. Besides, this is ten times better than rotting away six feet under somewhere. Don't you think?"

"Trust me," Maria mumbles, taking short, careful steps forward in the soft light. She turns toward the never-ending tunnel of a space and runs her hand in the air. The air hums slightly under her touch, sending a soft vibration against her palm. "The condition your body was in when I found you . . ." She looks at Luna to see if she's bothered about Maria bringing up Luna's death. A confident smile on her face,

Luna raises her eyebrows, gesturing for Maria to go on. "Yeah, girl. The only thing your earthly torso is good for now is worm food."

Maria catches the pillow Luna's tossed at her. At least her reflexes still work here. Or is it training? Maria's not sure. Holding onto the pillow, she runs her fingers over its soft fabric and continues investigating the strange world she's entered.

"Must you be so morbid all the time?" Luna asks, trying to sound annoyed. But it's clear that Luna's in good spirits. How could she not be? Living alone with Laura Solomon in this mindfuck of a place must be a real pickle.

Maria lowers her hand and stares into space. Too many questions run through her mind at once. She wants answers to all of them, but she's here for a specific reason. And who knows how long she has before Laura will send her ass back down to the mansion?

Luna beats her to it. "Are you in a stasis capsule right now?"

Maria takes the strides that separate her from Luna and tosses the pillow at her. Luna dodges, and the pillow lands softly against the purple bedding. "No, I'm not in a capsule. Can't you see me from here? I thought you and Solomon spy on us day in and day out."

"If there's a camera nearby, we can see you. But I think Dennis and Bill took those down a long time ago."

"A camera?" Maria crosses her arms. "I thought you were like . . . almighty and shit."

"We are. Or I guess Laura is, and I will be. Once I'm done with my training."

Maria raises her eyebrows in surprise.

"Yeah, I know," Luna says, amusement glimmering in her clear, shining eyes. "Not exactly the most cheerful of mentors I have." She gestures at the door with the white glow under it. "But Laura is becoming the most complex supercomputer out there. So I'm letting it slide—her not being all puppies, hugs, and butterflies."

"If she's a computer, doesn't that mean she's . . . "

"Dead? Yeah, I keep asking that. But no. All the data is still integrated with her mind. In a way, it's not that different from being Chipped and existing in the AR."

"And that brings me to why I'm here," Maria says, standing taller and letting her hands fall by her side. "I need answers about the Unchipped."

Luna blinks a few times, staring at Maria with curiosity. Does she have to blink? Can she suffer from dry eyes here? Why does she even have eyes? A face?

She gets up from the bed to stand in front of Maria. "Shoot."

"What?" Maria's momentarily lost under all the questions rushing through her mind.

"You said you have questions. Let's hear them."

"Right." Maria sits on the mattress, surprised to feel a real, firm bed under her body. "Bill tried to ask Solomon about it. We need to know what makes us, well, what we are."

Luna nods. "You mean what makes Unchipped people Unchipped?"

"Bingo."

"Why do you need to know?"

"We're going to go through with it. Margaret's plan. The dechipping. Texas is working on getting his guy over from the green city as we speak."

"His *guy*?"

"The surgeon. Baldwin. He can remove our chips, but we need to get him and his team smuggled into the mansion without anyone in the program noticing."

"I thought the mansion wasn't safe."

"It isn't. Nowhere is. Not with these things," Maria taps the side of her head, "stuck in our brains. No, we need to dechip first and then leave the mansion."

Luna's face becomes serious. She pauses to bite her lower lip. "You sure about this?"

"What do you mean, am I sure? Luna, they sent a missile to kill you and Jovan. A single drone can put you down just by playing a deadly tune. They can hack into Markus's or Dennis's brain and tell them to jump off the roof. Yes, my friend. I'm pretty damn sure I want this thing out of my head."

Luna swallows and dodges Maria's gaze. She looks down at the floor and clears her throat. "Yeah, but every coin has a flip side."

"Okay." Maria frowns. "And what's the flip side?"

"I'm saying that dechipping is risky too."

"I already told you, we have City of California's best surgeon—"

"Not that. A different kind of risk."

Maria inhales sharply, slowly losing her temper. This place, this conversation, the information over-load . . . it's driving her toward a meltdown. "What risk, Luna?"

She gestures around her. "Well, you'd never be able to visit me again."

"That's not a risk."

"Yeah, well . . . " Luna turns her face away. "It's still true."

"Don't take this the wrong way," Maria says between her teeth. "But this is not exactly a pleasure trip for me. I'm glad you're not dead, I really am. And I miss you, Lu. We all do. But I'm still *alive*-alive. So are Bill and Kaarina and everyone else. And we're doing our best to keep it that way."

Luna looks away again, something sad shadowing her face. "But I'm not dead."

Maria exhales and gives Luna a half-smile. "You know what I mean. I mean, you chose to come here and work with Solomon. Isn't that what you wanted all along?"

Without replying, Luna turns to pace around the mattress. Deep in her thoughts, she seems to have forgotten that Maria is there.

"Luna, I don't know if I have much time. I need to know about the Unchipped issue."

"So you can all dechip and live happily ever after."

"Yes."

"And forget that I ever existed."

"Luna. Come on. This is not like you. What's going on?"

Halfheartedly, she kicks the mattress. In frustration, she extends her hands. "I'm just saying that there's another option."

"Dying and uploading?"

Luna opens her mouth to reply, but no words come out.

Maria takes a deep breath. "So what are you suggesting here? Should I go back down and tell the crew that . . . what? Hey guys, Luna wouldn't tell me what makes the Unchipped Unchipped, but she offered to off us all and slice our brain so we can live in a yellow room with a bunch of dogs?"

Luna keeps staring at her, not saying a word.

"Can you imagine Bill's reaction? Or freaking Yeti's?" Maria says, rolling her eyes. "So pack your bags, guys," she continues with an overly cheerful voice, "we're moving in with Solomon and Luna in the egg. Plenty of room for everyone. And don't worry about Solomon, she mostly just sulks alone in a corner like she's in a timeout. Or braindead. Not sure what, because she's not talking to anyone anymore. But never mind that; Luna has a million fake dogs for us to play with, and we all get our own shitty mattress to sleep—"

"Stop mocking my room!" Luna yells suddenly.

Maria's hand freezes in the air. Her lips are still moving, but no sound comes out. She turns to stare at Luna in horror. She tries to apologize, but her words are silent. Panicked and out of breath, Maria stares at Luna, pointing at her mouth.

Luna takes a deep breath and closes her eyes. Then she turns some invisible volume button Maria can't see, and suddenly her words have sound again.

"Did you just . . ." Maria gasps, out of breath. "Did you just put me on *mute*?"

"I just want you to . . ."

Maria lifts her hand and gestures Luna to give her a moment. She shouldn't have said all those things to Luna. She's out of line. But being stuck in the mansion, waiting for the killer drones, missiles, and sonic weapons has started to take its toll.

Hurt flickers in Luna's eyes. "I know I opted for this. To live and work here with Laura. I thought I'd be happy here. That this was what I wanted. But I guess I'm just . . ." She bites her lower lip. "I'm lonely here, Maria. I can't even tap you guys to chitchat, like we did before."

Maria regrets her words even more, suddenly wishing she was still on mute. "Sorry. Lu, I didn't mean all that. I'm sorry."

She waves Maria off, but the hurt is still evident on her face. "Can you just keep an open mind?" Luna says.

"Open mi . . ." Maria presses her lips together and stops talking before she lashes out again. It doesn't help anyone for her to piss off Luna. The girl has always had a temper, and no matter how idiotic her suggestion for everyone to just *die*, Maria still loves her. She nods at Luna, gesturing that she'll think about it.

"That was a dick move, by the way."

"What was?" Luna asks and sits down on the mattress, burying her face in her hands. Regret washes over Maria. How lonely she must feel here. Alone. Dead. No wonder she wants everyone here with her. Maria would, too, if she were in Luna's shoes.

"Your little mute button trick."

"Mm."

Maria throws her hands in the air and exhales deeply. "Fine. I'll talk to them. The guys. I'll let them know your idea. Okay?"

Luna looks up, new hope brightening her face.

"But first, you need to get me that information. We need to know that it's safe for us to dechip. That it's not going to kill us for real. Nobody's removed a chip from an Unchipped brain before. I'm not sure if it's been done for Chipped individuals either."

"I'll talk to Laura," Luna says. "If she won't tell me, at least she can give me access to the chipping research files."

Maria exhales and closes her eyes. "Thank you."

"And you'll talk to them? About uploading?"

Maria keeps her eyes closed. She needs to play this well, or she'll lose Luna's help. Opening her eyes, she sits down on the mattress next to Luna and elbows her playfully. "I'll start with Yeti. And I'll make sure to take note of how many times Bill says 'Jesus on a bike' when he hears your message."

Luna chuckles but then falls quiet again. She turns her face away to hide her expression.

"Hey, come on." Maria bumps her again. "That pout of yours is more serious than Sanna's."

Luna scoffs but can't help her smile. "How is she? Does she still have that critter?"

"Mhm. Mister Bun Bun is very much alive and well. Just like Sanna."

"And Kaarina? Does she still sneak into Yeti's room every night, thinking we have no idea what's going on?"

Maria laughs. "She really would make the worst spy. I can hear her heel-walking from the other end of the hallway."

Luna's laughter seems to brighten the whole room. Grinning, she looks at Maria and nods at her. "I know my suggestion is a lot to process."

"Hey, I'd die for you in a heartbeat, girl. Just not before I turn eighty-five."

Luna frowns but keeps smiling. "That's awfully specific."

Maria shrugs. "That's when my *abuela* went. And she wanted to go. It was like she decided to turn off a switch, and she was gone. Deciding when you die, that's true freedom, if you ask me."

"How old are you now?" Luna asks, a genuinely curious expression on her face.

"I thought you weren't supposed to ask a lady her age?" Maria jokes.

"Ha! You're no lady," Luna says, covering her face from Maria's pillow attack. "A lady would never beat her younger and smaller peer."

Maria chuckles and lets Luna grab the pillow. "I'm thirty . . . " With a puzzled look on her face, Maria looks up at the yellow ceiling. "Holy shitballs, I've lost count! Thirty-five? Thirty-six?"

One of the dogs jogs over and sits between Maria and Luna next to the mattress. Luna reaches for its neck, scratching the dog under its collar. "Well, if you want to die at eighty-five sharp, I'd keep better count. Because after your previous vacation in the stasis capsule, the mirror won't help you figure it out."

Maria frowns. "What kind of a sick riddle is that supposed to be?"

"Not a riddle. I may not know everything about the Unchipped brain scans, but I have learned a thing or two during my time with our ice queen."

"Such as? We already know the capsules heal people. I mean, look at Jovan. He was well on his way when Ef and I got him in that pod. And now he's nearly ready to come out and keep going like he never wrestled with a freaking missile."

"Do you also know that those pods stop you from aging?"

Maria blinks. A sudden adrenaline spike rushes through her head. "Wouldn't that make us . . . "

"Immortal?" Luna shakes her head. "Not at all. But the nanobots do refresh your system. No need to worry about gray hairs and wrinkles."

More blinking. That's all she can do. Is she going to be young forever?

Luna jumps up from the mattress and offers her hand to Maria. "Don't just sit there blinking. Come."

Again, Maria's too puzzled to refuse Luna's overly intimate gesture. Maria's never been a hugger, or a hand holder. But now, she takes Luna's hand and lets her walk her deeper into the yellow tunnel. Soon, they stop, seemingly in the middle of . . . nothing.

"Luna, I'm losing my mind here. No more games."

"I know it's a lot." Luna turns and taps the air, and a small screen appears. Luna starts tapping it with both hands, her fingers flying on the see-through surface. "Just one more thing, I swear. Then I'll let you go."

Maria opens her mouth to object but doesn't have time. A door with a green and black glow appears out of thin air. Luna places her hand on the door's shimmering surface and looks at Maria over her shoulder. "You ready?"

"Ready for what? To see your walk-in closet?"

Luna grins and pushes the door. "Nope, nothing to do with me." A click sounds, and the door swooshes aside. "This is *your* room."

Maria steps deeper into what looks like a cyber desert with random furniture and gadgets in a green glow. A shiny limo with tinted windows, closets filled with guns and knives, wardrobes with all black clothing . . .

"What . . . wha . . . " Maria has no words.

"This is the first time I've ever heard you stutter."

"That's because I don't do that."

"Okay."

"And you've never lived with me."

"I've lived in your head. Which is much nicer than being in Bill's mind, I must say."

Maria walks over to one of the open closets. She picks up a samurai sword. "Solomon created this place?"

"No, I did."

Maria turns and stares at Luna in awe. "According to what data exactly?"

"No data."

"What, then?"

Luna shrugs and takes the samurai sword from Maria, investigating its shiny surface. "Just a handful of assumptions and educated guesses."

"*This* is how you see me?"

Luna extends the sword before her and whooshes it through the air. The green flow hums and vibrates softly. "Yup. You're a badass."

Maria huffs, spinning slowly in place. This is nothing like her. Nothing like what she enjoys. It's as far off from *home* as can be. "And what is that noise? In the background?"

Luna taps the air and turns yet another invisible volume button. "It's rap. Obviously."

Maria listens to the Spanish words, gesturing for Luna to turn it down. "Chicano? Come on, girl."

Luna turns the music down. "I can play whatever you want. Just name it. Grupera? Danza?"

"Let's not." Maria shakes her head at Luna but can't help laughing at her enthusiasm. "Just stop, okay? You know I don't listen to this shit."

Luna taps the air, and a new tune fills the space around them.

"Mariachi?" This time Maria bends over, holding her stomach as she laughs. "I'm telling you, Luna, this must be the most racist moment of my life."

The music stops. "Oh, no. No, I'm just teasing you."

Maria waves her off. "I know you don't always know how to deal with . . . well, *people*."

Luna walks to Maria, smiles, and turns to face the same direction as Maria. "But seriously, I can make it whatever you want. Anything. Create your own paradise with zero problems, stress-free days, and yummy food. Hell, I can even create a dream date for you. Whatever you want them to look like, sound like, feel like—"

"Okay, that shit is just creepy. Like, AR-companion creepy."

Luna lifts her finger, gesturing for Maria to hold on. "Don't mock it until . . ." The rest of her sentence turns into a murmur. After a minute or two of Luna fiddling with numerous screens—which appear out of the vibrating air—she takes a step back, a wide smile on her face.

"Okay, what's that shit-eating grin about?" Maria crosses her arms and raises her eyebrows at Luna.

"Turn around." Luna nods at something behind Maria.

Without turning, Maria closes her eyes in frustration. "I swear, if I turn around and there's a mariachi band behind me—"

"Hello." The man's voice is silky and low. The air around Maria's face vibrates smoothly as he speaks. "You must be Maria."

She opens her eyes but doesn't turn around.

"Luna tells me you're feeling lonely."

Maria shakes her head. Dry laughter escapes her lips. Finally, she turns around and faces the most beautiful man she's ever seen in her life. He takes a step closer and smiles.

Maria lifts her hand. "Nope."

The man stops and tilts his head slightly. "I just want to introduce . . ."

"Yeah, no. Mm-m." Maria stands her ground, her arms crossed against her chest. "Not going to happen."

"If you just let me . . ."

"Nope. Nope. Nope. Luna." She turns around to give Luna a dirty look. "You've had your fun. Just make him go away now, okay?"

"Did I get it wrong?"

"What?"

"Too pretty?"

Maria looks over her shoulder. She needs to remind herself that the *thing* standing behind her has no feelings, so he can't be offended.

"Okay, here. How about now?"

Maria turns back around. A broad-chested man with a rough beard and smoky bedroom eyes stares at her, a teasing half-smile lingering on his handsome face.

"What the hell is wrong with you?" Maria says with a raised voice. Though she's talking to Luna, she can't take her eyes off of the smoking-hot algorithm standing in front of her.

"Ah," Luna says from behind her. "Now I get it. Silly me, I should have known. Just . . . here."

The muscular man changes shape in front of Maria's eyes. Vibrating and glowing a white light, the man glitches and changes into a gorgeous woman with short hair, partly shaved on one side. A flower tattoo starts from her cheek and leads down onto her neck and under her black T-shirt. The woman narrows her eyes and smiles. "You must be Ma . . ."

"Okay." Maria stomps over to Luna. Without knowing what she's doing, she starts to tap and swipe the see-through screens and keyboards hovering in the air. "You won't stop this madness? I'll stop it myself."

Luna bursts out laughing, trying to push Maria away from her gadgets. "Okay, okay, hey. You're doing it wrong."

The woman with the tattoo glitches again and changes into a half-man, half-woman with a summer dress, floating in the wind. Then it turns into a yellow lab, panting and wagging its tail until Luna tap-taps the air determinedly. The creature in front of them disappears.

"Good lord, woman," Maria says. "That's a fucked-up party trick right there."

"Maybe next time you just tell me what you want?"

Maria closes her eyes briefly and fights to keep her grin. "I'm sorry . . . *Next* time?"

The sudden bright light temporarily blinds Maria. With narrowed eyes, she looks at the silhouette standing in the doorway. White light shines around Doctor Solomon, making it hard to see her. Against the white lab coat, Laura's holding something firm. An object which Maria faintly recognizes.

A chipping helmet.

"Time's up, chica."

Luna and Maria stare at Solomon, then at each other, both of their mouths open and too surprised to reply. Luna recovers first.

"Was that . . . a joke?"

Solomon steps in and looks around the green and black space, a bored look on her face. "Hardly a joke. As far as I know, Maria here is a real-life girl, and chica just means—"

"We know what chica means, Laura." Luna rolls her eyes. "I'm just proud of you for finally discovering the wonder of pet names. Good for you, Doc."

Maria takes a few steps closer to Solomon. It's hard to not think of all the terrible things the woman's done in her lifetime. How she murdered thousands of innocent people and turned many more into scientific experiments, Maria included. But she needs to keep her calm. Because as much as she hates Solomon, they need her more than ever. She clears her throat and nods at the helmet. "What's up with that?"

A shrug. "You know what this is?"

Maria blows air through her lips. "Do I know . . ." *Bitch please*, she thinks but stops herself from calling Solomon names. "Yeah, your minions shoved me in a stasis capsule a while back. Remember? Good times."

"Okay, good," Laura says dryly. She turns and walks back into the white glow, leaving the door open.

Maria and Luna stare after her. When Luna walks back into the egg, Maria hurries to follow her. No way in hell does she want to stay alone in any of these rooms. Who knows what kind of sexy monster will flash into life next?

Back in the egg, Laura sits down in one of three chairs in the middle of the room. Luna follows and sits down next to her, but Maria hesitates. She stays behind, hovering by the doorway. She crosses her arms and lifts her chin. "Is the helmet for me? To get back down to the mansion?"

Laura glances at her, momentarily puzzled. "How would it take you back to the mansion?"

"Can you please just tell me what's up?" Maria has to work to keep her voice calm.

"Your plan. Dechipping." Laura lifts the helmet up. "You can use the helmet to do it. I'll send Baldwin a memo on how to reverse the chipping process."

Suspicion isn't something Maria should feel in this moment; she should be feeling relief. She stares at the helmet in Laura's hands, realizing then that it's just an image. Just a demonstration. Like everything else up here.

"Okay . . . " She pauses to think. "But that'll only work for the Chipped? Dennis, Markus, Jenny, and

Owena? How about the rest of us? Is it safe for an Unchipped person to use?"

Solomon shrugs. "There's only one way to find out."

"Are you shitting me right now?" Maria says, her voice filled with rage.

"Whoa, okay." Luna stands up and raises her hands. "Let's take a step back here. I'm sure Laura has more information to give you. About the helmet and the Unchipped. So let's hear her out, okay?" Luna sits back down and taps on the chair next to her.

After a long exhale, Maria drags her feet to the chair and sits down. She dodges their looks. This place is ridiculous. It's not even real, yet here they sit, making decisions for those who cut and bleed.

Laura sits taller, staring Maria down. "I can't tell you what you want to hear—"

"Because Sanna wouldn't visit you here?" Maria gives her a mocking smile. "That's bullshit, and you know it."

Laura takes a breath and pauses for a long time. A neutral expression on her face, she moves her head back and looks down her nose at Maria. "I can't tell you, because I don't have all the data."

"More horse shit." Maria scoffs. "You've dug around Unchipped brains for years now. There's no way you don't know what we are."

"Sure, I've done a lot of research. But during my time, in order to map a brain, we needed to carve off slivers of brain to develop detailed pictures of the brain's wiring. We'd then stick the images back together but, goes without saying, the test subject cannot be put under the electron microscope like this and then be brought back to life."

Luna and Maria both stare at Solomon, lost for words.

"You can look at me like I'm a scientist gone mad all you want. It's simply called connectomics, and it's nothing more than neuroscientists trying to crack the human genome."

Maria raises her eyebrows at Solomon. "And this is what happened to Margaret Lewis?"

"Yes. But Lewis was killed by Nurse Saarinen. Not me."

"Oh, okay. So you expect me to believe that you never killed an Unchipped test subject to figure out what goes on in their brain?"

Laura presses her lips into a thin line before she answers. "If they weren't already as good as dead?" She shrugs. "No, I never killed anyone."

"So the slicing or scanning, or whatever the fuck you call it, won't tell you why our brains can't be integrated with the CS?"

"No, it does."

Maria stands up so fast that the chair falls behind her. The dull *thump* sound distracts her from her anger. She looks back, just to see if the chair is still there.

"Hold on," Luna says. "If what you're saying is true—"

"Of course it's true," says Laura in her matter-of-fact voice. "I have no reason to lie about this. I don't care enough to lie about this."

"You don't care? Really?" Maria pauses when it hits her: she's telling the truth. It explains why Laura's been unavailable and harder and harder to reach, even as the rebels implement the plan Laura herself devised. This place . . . Doctor Solomon is losing her grip on reality. "But your daughter," she reminds Laura. "She'll die too, if this shit goes wrong."

"I know that. And that's why I want her here instead. Dennis knows my instructions. He's the guardian of Sanna as long as she's down there and I'm up here. And Jenkins knows better than to go against my will."

"Dennis hasn't said a word about Sanna not getting dechipped." Maria stares at Solomon in disbelief. Would Texas really keep something this big from her?

"I know he hasn't."

"And why the fuck not?"

"Because it's none of your business."

Maria kicks the chair twice. It moves slowly away from her and then disappears into the white glow.

"Yeah, that's useless," Luna says to Maria. "Kick all you want, but it's not going to break. Trust me. I've tried."

Maria turns her back to hide her frustration. She stares at a map of a city she vaguely recognizes—a place with blinking lights and tall buildings.

"Back to this slicing business," Luna says. "If what you said is true . . ."

"It is true."

"Oh for Pete's sake, will you let me finish my sentence?" Luna's voice echoes slightly in the space around them. To Maria's surprise, Solomon raises her hands and gestures for Luna to go on.

"You never sliced an Unchipped brain."

"No, I haven't." She pauses for two seconds. "Not me personally. I had men to do it and each time they did, the process itself succeeded, but whereas the normal human brain has more than a hundred billion neurons and millions of miles of wires, the Unchipped brain has even more. To map your brain," Solomon nods at Maria, "is a daunting task, to say the least."

Luna hurries to talk before Maria can recover from her fury and lash out at Solomon. "Okay, but we know that Nurse Saarinen has done it successfully at least once."

"She's done it multiple times. Like I said, it's not the slicing that is the problem. It's what comes after. But if anyone could have made progress on this, it would be Nurse Saarinen. They don't take the Unchipped prisoner or use them for processing power anymore. Where Nurse Saarinen is coming from, your people are for testing—and testing only."

"So she knows." Maria finds her voice again. "She knows, and we don't."

Laura stands up from the chair, walks over to Maria, and hands the chipping helmet to her. "You say that like it's a bad thing, if she knows."

Stunned, Maria accepts the chipping helmet and stares at Laura with bewildered eyes. "The murderous maniac, who has more power than anyone else in the world, holds the one piece of information we need to stay alive. That's not a bad thing, in your opinion?"

Laura taps the helmet before she turns to walk away. As she heads toward another strange door, leading to who knows what fuckery, her voice booms in the white nothingness. "Not necessarily, chica. Not necessarily."

The dark night opens in front of them through the mansion's front door. Somewhere in the distance, rusty gates creak open. Soon, four wheels crunch their way across the gravel. Maria stands next to a hand-twisting Kaarina, a teeth-grinding Yeti, and Bill, tapping his bare foot nervously against the front hallway's floor.

Markus, Micky, and Dennis hover somewhere near the pantry. The girls are upstairs playing some kind of a game that involves a creepy-looking porcelain doll. They've come down several times, begging Dennis to find them a metal bucket. Dennis told them no. More often than not, Dennis is the only one who isn't willing to give the girls a free range to do whatever they want. It makes Maria like the man a bit more.

"And she's sure about the hack?" Bill asks for the eleventh time.

Maria gives him a tired look. "Can you please stop asking me that? You sound like a cracker-craving parrot."

"I just don't see how Solomon can hack into any of that shit when they couldn't even save Margaret on that operating table."

"You'd needs thumbs for that," Kaarina mumbles, her eyes locked on the black limo sliding to a stop.

"Thumbs?" Bill makes a face. "Girl, what are you on about?"

"A computer can't lift a person off a table to save her life." Yeti's voice is surprisingly calm. He usually doesn't have that kind of patience with Bill. Or anyone, for that matter. "A computer also can't slap a maniac nurse in the face or knock her out cold. But a computer *can* hack into another computer and steal the information we need."

Bill shakes his head, then tucks a dreadlock back behind his ear. "Shit's too crazy. Lulu the computer. Man, she must be going mad in that hellhole. Can you imagine? Being stuck in a freaking egg with Doctor fucking Solomon?" Bill shakes the thought off. "Not no, but hell no."

A man in a black suit steps out of the limo. The driver stays in the car, the electric vehicle humming steadily. Dennis walks past them to the porch. After a quick glance up to the sky, he walks to Doctor Baldwin with his hand extended. "Robert. Good to see you."

"Dennis." The two men shake hands, and Robert gestures at the limo. "Can Quinn stay with us for the night?"

Dennis looks puzzled. "Just Quinn? Where's Jenny? She told me she'd come home with the rest of the medical crew . . . " Dennis looks even more puzzled. "And I don't see the crew either. What's going on?"

Doctor Baldwin lifts a finger and walks to the back of the car. He knocks on the trunk twice. The trunk opens, and Baldwin picks up something from inside. A stack of chipping helmets.

"I don't know about Jenny. And no crew needed, just these. Solomon's orders."

"So she did call you."

"Email. Is it true what they say about her?"

"I don't know, Robert." Dennis gestures for Baldwin to follow him inside. He glances up at the sky, trying to hide his worry. "What do they say?"

"That she's a ghost in the machine?"

"More like a huge pain in the ass," Maria says and steps aside, giving room to the two men. Baldwin turns to look at her. "Maria. Looking good." He points at his temple. "How's the head?"

Maria gives him a quick, forced smile. "Still attached."

The doctor laughs. "And that's why I'm here. To keep it that way." He turns to shake Bill's hand. "Good to see you, William. I hear you got yourself promoted. No more designing goods for the AR-catalog, then?"

Bill lets go of his hand and gestures for them to move to the kitchen. "Nah, man. But I gotta say, drawing shit like see-through banana backpacks or pink pet goat-penguins was sometimes just as challenging as saving the world."

"You don't say?"

Just as they sit down around the kitchen table, two pairs of running feet rattle the spiral staircase. Owena's serious face peeks out from the doorway, then Sanna's.

"Can we go out and burn Tina's hair in a metal bucket?"

They all blink and stare at Owena, trying to process her request.

Kaarina recovers first, shaking her head slightly in confusion. "What? No. And who's Tina?"

Before the girl can answer, Bill turns to Kaarina. "What do you mean, 'Who's Tina?' What difference does it make who the fuck Tina is? No, they're not allowed to torch *anyone's* head!"

Kaarina glares at Bill and looks at Maria for support. She shrugs a shoulder. "Gotta say. I'm with Billy-boy on this one."

"Not her whole head," Owena continues, her face stern. "Just the hair. We found a box of mat—"

"Go back upstairs, kid." Yeti waves them off. "We'll go shoot rats in the barnyard or something once we're done here."

"The fuck?" Bill throws his hands up in the air. "Nobody's shooting anyone. No living creature dies on my watch."

"So . . . " Sanna says, frowning. "Go back to our room?"

"Yes, child!" Bill snaps. "And take your doll-burning comrade with you."

Maria watches, muffling her laughter, as the two kids sneak away. But instead of heading to the spiral staircase, they crack open the pantry in the hallway and fill their pockets with what's left of the raw chocolate bars. She shakes her head and rolls her eyes as the kids grin at her on their way back upstairs. Once they're gone, Maria's left with a restless thought that stops her from focusing on the ongoing conversation.

Why hasn't Jenny come home with more food?

"That's it?" Markus's elevated voice snaps Maria back to this time and place. "As soon as we know the specifics of this HSP thing, we can all be chip-free?"

Baldwin nods. "You yourself don't have to wait that long. I can operate on you tonight if you want me to." He nods again, this time at Dennis. "Mister Jenkins too."

"But not us?" Micky asks, a flustered look on his face. "Why not us?"

"I could proceed with the reverse chipping process for an Unchipped person too," Baldwin says. "But Doctor Solomon says there's a risk. Though I've got to say, after going through the highly sensitive person brain maps, and learning about the dechipping through helmets, I do not see what she sees. I agree with her about the Unchipped mind mapping issue, that we simply don't have enough petabytes to store all the data collection. But we're not mind mapping here, we're removing a microchip from the brain cortex. Why Doctor Solomon feels so strongly about these two completely different scenarios being somehow a threat to one another . . . like I said. I'm not sure I see what she sees."

"With all due respect, doc," Yeti says, "Laura Solomon is not exactly a mother hen. If she's worried, it's not because she's overly cautious. It's because the data says there's an issue. A risk."

"Fair enough." Baldwin reaches over for a water bottle on the table. He tries to twist the cap open, but it remains stuck. "So we wait for this hack to take place and get whatever information Nurse Saarinen has about this disorder of yours."

"It's not a disorder." Maria reaches for the bottle in Baldwin's hands, twists the cap open, and hands it back to him.

"My mistake. I misspoke." Baldwin takes a gulp of water. "This condition."

"Not a condition, either," Bill says. "Dehydration is a condition. Bipolarity is a disorder. I've experienced both, and none of this HSP bullshit is anything like that. I mean, highly sensitive?" With both hands, Bill wildly gestures at the Yeti sitting next to him. "*This* guy?"

"Oh, go pound sand, Yankee."

Bill grins at the big man. "Aw, nicknames."

"Okay," Maria says, rolling her eyes at Kaarina. She taps the woman while waiting for the bickering and joking to subside. *Like I said . . . a pack of bitches in heat, these guys.*

Kaarina grins at Maria. *"Your monkeys. Your circus."*

"Let's focus here," Maria says to everyone at the table. "I say we get this over and done with for those who are safe to have the procedure. So Dennis, Markus, and Owena."

Dennis clears his throat. "Robert, did you happen to see Jenny in the city?"

"Your assistant?" He shakes his head briefly. "No. Was I supposed to?"

"I better make an AR-call," Dennis says and gets up. "I'm all down for this dechipping plan, but I do need to tell Jenny what's going on."

An excited voice echoes through the hallway, coming from the spiral staircase. "Are you coming out with us, Mister Jenkins?"

Bill raises his head. "Get back to your room, Sanna. You are not going outside. I swear, if I need to tell you one more time, there'll be no pancakes for you for the rest of the week."

Quick footsteps run up the stairs. Dennis follows the girl upstairs, where the AR-glasses await. He will have to convince Owena to get the surgery too, but somehow Maria's not worried that the girl will be against the idea. The helmet alone would be such an interesting gadget to her that she would probably agree to the operation.

Maria nods at Markus. "How about you? Feel like a guinea pig yet?"

The Chipped man runs his hand through his overgrown hair and gives Maria a small smile. "I've had my head poked and chip hacked by the Happiness-Program enough for this lifetime. And I'm tired of running from their drones. This chip is the worst thing that ever happened to me." He glances in Kaarina's direction, then quickly looks at Maria again. "I'll go first. And I'll go tonight."

Two portable operating tables stand in the middle of the hallway. The front door is open, and Dennis's driver, Quinn, wheels in metal boxes, screens, and scanners, and finally—a tall stack of chipping helmets.

Maria stands by the doorway, fidgeting with her headphones. Something about the murky sky puts her on edge. The green glow in the distance raises a lump in her throat, and the light against the night sky seems more vibrant than it's ever been. Maybe it is.

Maybe I'm losing my mind.

Yeti hovers near the operating table while Kaarina and Markus half-whisper to one another. Markus sits on the table, holding a chipping helmet in his hands. Baldwin clears out wires and taps on the screens. Dennis stares into one with charts and numbers running on a black background. He's been quiet—more so than usual—ever since he gave up on tracking down Jenny in the city.

"Did you contact Ef?" Bill had asked Dennis repeatedly. And each time Dennis nodded, never losing his temper. "Yes, son. He hasn't seen Jenny since she left with the boxes of food two days ago." A sad, worried look deepened on his face.

"But she has those chicks she hangs out with," Bill kept ranting, wildly gesturing with his hand. "The alley bitches, or something like that?"

"She does. But I can't reach her goddess friends either."

Maria can't help but smile when she stares at Dennis, who's now moving on to monitor the screen nearest Markus and the operating table. Not too long ago, she had been ready to rip the chip out of his brain with her bare hands. Not to dechip the man, but to kill him. Without Solomon's plan to use Dennis by making him the lead man of the Happiness-Program, Maria probably would have torn his little head off his broad shoulders. And now, she's actually . . . almost fond of the man. Not romantically—she shakes her head to banish the thought—but still. Dennis Jenkins has become one of the good ones. Who would have guessed?

Maria spins around at a sudden movement behind her. Before she can stop herself, her hand closes around Quinn's throat. The woman gasps, her eyes wide.

"Don't startle people like that," Maria says, still holding onto the driver's throat.

"Fi . . ." Quinn struggles to speak under Maria's grip. "Fire."

She lets go of Quinn. "What?! Where?"

Quinn looks panicked. She waves fiercely toward the front door. "It's . . ." a cough attack stops her from talking.

"It's what?! Out at the barn?"

Quinn coughs while rubbing her throat. "Yes." She stops to cough some more. "It's still far off, but one of the stalls is in full flames."

For two seconds, Maria's mind blanks out. Then, a sense of urgency rushes through her.

"Tina's hair," she mumbles. She gazes at the spiral staircase, then the mansion's open front door. "Sneaky little fuckers . . ." She huffs and takes off toward the pantry where Dennis keeps the fire extinguisher.

"Hey, whoa!" Dennis's voice booms behind her. "What's going on?"

Maria shoves off her headphones and lets them fall around her neck. "They snuck out!"

"Who snuck out?" Micky asks, but quickly he seems to realize who.

"And they've started a fire," Maria says coolly to Dennis, her training kicking in. The panic fades away, and a smooth calmness takes over. She grabs the fire extinguisher and heads back toward the front door.

"A fire?" Dennis blinks and stares out the door. "The doll," he says, and steps out onto the porch to look around.

"It's at the barn," Maria says, taking a step out, but then back into the building again. She places the headphones back on. She's on autopilot now. All her senses scream at her not to leave the mansion. She shouldn't be outside. No one should. Something's off.

An uneasy vibration in the air.

A buzzing feeling.

Do feelings have a buzzing sound?

"Something's not right," Maria says, staring out the door. "Not just the fire. Nobody goes outside."

Dennis nods at her. "You're afraid of the sonic weapon. I'll go get the girls. You stay here."

"No," Maria grabs Dennis by his sleeve. "You're not safe, either. If there's a drone, it might carry the sonic weapon and attack the Unchipped, but they might also locate and destroy the Chipped. Remember what Iris said? No firewall will help you if the drone identifies and has direct access to you."

Dennis takes Maria by the shoulders. "I don't see any drones out there." He lets go and gives her a warm smile. "I'll be fine, doll."

Maria pauses and looks over her shoulder. But before she has time to assess the situation further, Dennis has made his way outside and disappeared around the corner.

"What the . . . " She takes a step further out but then stops. "I just told him not to—"

Before Maria can stop him, Yeti grabs the fire extinguisher from her and pushes out the door. "The fire," he calls over his shoulder, "I'll deal with it while Dennis finds the girls." Yeti is gone before Maria has time to argue with him.

Cursing, Maria returns inside to grab her sniper rifle. Everyone else is gathered near the windows, watching her with alert eyes. A small shadow makes its way down the stairs, hopping down onto the hallway floor. The rabbit stands on its hind feet, looking around the room.

Maria gestures at the rabbit, then at everyone else. "Every single being in this house stays inside," she says and then walks back to the door, but hesitates to step onto the porch. The warning—a gut feeling—overrides her other thoughts. This feeling is not unfamiliar to her, she'd recognize it in her sleep.

An enemy approaching.

Just as Maria lifts her rifle to scan the night sky, Kaarina's scream fills the room. "A drone!" she yells and leaves the side window where she's been scanning the yard. "If the drone identifies Dennis, he's going to get hacked!"

"I know that," Maria says back to Kaarina and lifts the rifle on her shoulder. "I just told him that and off he went anyway. Stay inside. Put your headphones on and activate the microphone."

"Oh no, is Owena wearing her helmet or not?" Micky joins Kaarina's panic, both of them oblivious to Maria's instructions.

A soft thumping sound startles Maria, as she focuses to scan the sky. Sanna's rabbit. It hops down to the porch, down the stairs, and onto the driveway.

"I'll get him," Kaarina says and hurries toward the door.

Maria throws herself forward to stop Kaarina from leaving the mansion. "Wait, wait, wait," she says, raising her hands at them. "We have no idea what weapons this drone will have. Everyone back off. Leave the rabbit. Stay inside. Headphones on."

Baldwin and Micky do as they're told, but Kaarina dodges Maria and looks past her out the door. "But he's right there!"

"Back off, Kaarina. Just let me take care of it." As Maria adjusts her headphones, turns, and aims her rifle toward the approaching buzzing sound, Kaarina leaps past her and out the door. As she runs to the bunny, it spooks and runs further away from the mansion.

"No!" Markus yells after her and runs to the door. Maria blocks his way, still aiming at the sound and waiting for the drone to show itself. "Seriously, people. What is wrong with you? Stay. Inside. Nobody else goes out. Yeti or Dennis will bring Kaarina back along with the girls. And for the love of my sanity, would you *please* put your headphones on?"

Bill grabs a box and starts tossing out headphones to no one in particular. He looks around the room, then shoves a pair into Markus's hands too.

"The sonic weapon won't hurt me," Markus says, taking the headphones from Bill and setting them on the windowsill. Then he ducks past Maria and rushes out the door. Maria curses his name but continues to aim her weapon at the approaching drone. She still can't see it, but the buzzing sound has gotten stronger.

Markus is outside, yelling Kaarina's name. Kaarina can't hear him, though, because she's chasing Mister

Bun Bun down the road. Quinn shoves past Maria, heading toward the corner where Dennis had disappeared. "I need to go help Mister Jenkins," she says and storms out the door.

Maria lowers her rifle and stares at the chaotic scene outside. "What . . . the *actual* fuck!"

Quinn doesn't get far before the drone spots her. A red light flashes, and Quinn collapses to the ground, holding her head until she's lying lifeless on the gravel—blood running from her ears and pooling on the ground.

"What . . . " Micky breathes into the headphone's microphone.

"Her chip," Maria says calmly. "It's fried. Quinn's gone."

Maria lifts the rifle back on her shoulder and fires at the drone, but it dodges the bullet and moves out of sight, back toward the barn. She slides back the bolt and loads another cartridge into the chamber, exhales, waits.

Sanna appears from around the corner. She runs inside, holding onto her headphones. Tears streak her face. Owena follows closely behind, balancing the cage-hat on her head. The hat seems to protect her, just as they've hoped it would, because the drone doesn't scan her chip. Her eyes are tear-free, but a serious expression on her face makes her look years older. Owena walks in and heads straight toward the chairs. Sanna collapses against Maria, holding onto her tight with one hand while the other hand presses the headphones firmly against her ears. The girl's shirt is stained red.

"He just collapsed. Mister Jenkins. We couldn't get him to wake up. There was blood everywhere."

"Is Yeti with Dennis?" Maria asks the girl calmly.

"He . . ." Sanna stops to think. "He's at the barn. Putting out Tina's hair. Maria we . . . ." The girl's loud sob stops her from talking. "We didn't mean to . . ."

Maria reaches for the girl's head and strokes it. "I know, I know. We'll talk about it later. Okay? Go to Micky now. Stay out of sight and keep your headphones on."

The girl nods and leaves Maria's side.

Markus and Kaarina appear from around the corner.

"Quinn and Dennis are both gone," Maria yells at them. "The drone's attacking the Chipped. Get back in the house, now!"

Markus drags the sobbing Kaarina back toward the house, trying to place the headphones on her head.

Maria spies the drone as it approaches the mansion again. It hovers from the corner where Dennis lies lifeless, following Markus and Kaarina toward the mansion. The red scanning light that was the end of Quinn flickers on.

Maria curses in Spanish. "Markus! *Run!*" Maria steps outside and fires the rifle. The bullet barely hits the drone and glances off its side with a *ping* sound. She aims again but misses.

"Shit, shit, shit."

Markus releases Kaarina and grasps his head, agony twisting his face. Blood drips from his ears. Kaarina screams his name, but in reaching for Markus, she accidentally knocks her headphones loose.

Just as Maria decides to venture outside and drag Kaarina away from Markus, Yeti is already at her side, running back to the mansion from the barn. Carrying the fire extinguisher in one hand, the man picks Kaarina up with his free arm and carries her and the rabbit back into the mansion.

Maria aims again. She fires at the drone once. Twice. A third time. *Ping, ping, ping,* the bullets catapult off the buzzing drone as it deftly dips and dodges, avoiding all but the most minor damage. Finally, as the futility dawns on her, she lowers her weapon.

Maria stares at the drone in horror. Stares at Markus—lying in a pool of blood under a hovering drone. Slow and unnaturally steady, the drone lowers to Maria's eye level. There it mocks her. Stares at her. Challenges her.

All this time, she's been worried about the sonic weapon and Nurse Saarinen hacking into Owena's chip. She's underestimated the threat Markus and Dennis have been under. And now, just like that . . . they're both gone.

Maria forces a deep breath, then a step back.

She exhales.

Shuts her eyes.

And closes the door.

CHAPTER 5
THE REVENANT

The information rushes through her mind. Numbers, letters, folders, files—, it's all just a seething mass that becomes one with her thought process. Her mind.

Omnipotent. No access is denied. No information too complicated.

Laura stands on the edge of the void, staring down at the grid. Funny how she used to be scared of heights. The thought seems so childish right now. Useless. Weak.

Down below, the black emptiness tempts her.

Above her, a white glow keeps her grounded—stops her from jumping.

Nurse Saarinen's research files download into the database that is Laura's mind. No need to turn around and face the zeros and ones on the see-through wall. No need to type with her hands or breathe just for the sake of seeming more human. This is her. All of her. And there's no one here she needs to please or comfort . . .

"Snap out of your trance, doc."

Laura closes her eyes and suppresses a sigh.

"Something's going on at the mansion."

With slow steps, Laura turns her back to the void and looks up at the intruder. "Novak."

"Yes . . . " Luna frowns and takes an agitated step forward. "That's my name, all right. What's wrong with you?" Luna walks closer, snaps her fingers in front of Laura's face. The gesture seems to be in slow motion. Hazy.

"Okay, Laura. You're freaking me out. More than usual."

Hesitant and slightly agitated, Laura swipes the air three times. The wall behind Luna simmers down to a gray gloom. "What do you need this time?"

"Nice tone." Luna rolls her eyes at Laura's annoyance. "I guess you are still human, after all. Why else would you sound like such a bi—"

"Novak."

Luna stops in the middle of her sentence. She exhales sharply and says, "Something's going on at the mansion. I'm looking at the dechipping data, and nothing's coming in. It's all zeros, and none of the helmets have been used."

A halfhearted grunt escapes Laura's throat. Who cares what happens at the mansion? Dennis would keep her daughter . . . Laura cocks her head in temporary confusion. What's her daughter's name again? Laura focuses on the young girl's face, trying to remember.

"Sanna," she mumbles, momentarily lost in her own mind.

"That's right." Luna nods. "Think about Sanna. We should check on them, don't you think? I mean, even if Sanna is not getting the operation, Dennis Jenkins is. And if her guardian is in trouble . . ."

As Laura swipes at the wall and opens a new transparent screen, Luna's words fade. Silently, she focuses on Laura's typing. Learns the device she's about to hack.

For a while, they just stand there. Laura working, Luna watching.

"But I thought—"

"Hush."

Surprised that Luna doesn't argue, Laura continues to enter the code. Locating the device. Accessing the computer.

Like shoving a child into a stasis capsule, she thinks. *Lackluster response to a lackluster hack.*

"I thought the chipping helmets didn't have screens."

"They don't."

Soon, a new screen opens. A huge space with two operating tables fills the view in front of them.

The mansion's hallway.

Laura steps back to give Luna space, gesturing for her to take over.

"It's the vital signs monitor?" Luna asks but doesn't look at Laura. Her eyes are scanning the scene. Her rebel friends—sitting around the operating table with their chins tucked. Defeated. Hurt.

"Yes," Laura says. "The house is set up like a massive Faraday cage. But the equipment Baldwin brought with him for the dechipping is directly wired to the system in the van. If you know what you're looking for, you can find a way in."

"Can I talk to them?" Luna asks. And then, without waiting for Laura to answer the first question, "Where's Markus? And Dennis? I don't see them anywhere."

Laura walks back to the edge. The void is like a magnet, tickling her consciousness. Constantly pulling. Luring. Hands folded behind her back, she leans carefully over the edge. *Wonder what's down there.*

There's a soft *thud* against the back of Laura's neck. It doesn't hurt, whatever just hit her, but she can still feel its impact on her. She turns around. It's a . . . a shoe?

"Don't make me throw the other one," Luna says, her voice surprisingly calm. "This time, it'll land on your face."

Laura glances at the shoe, glances at Luna. With slow steps, she walks over to Luna's weapon of choice. While staring Luna straight in the eye, she kicks the shoe off the edge. It disappears into the void.

"Fine. Be that way. But before you shove me down too, I need audio."

"So access the speaker system on the power processor."

After opening her mouth for a snarky reply, Luna changes her mind. She turns to the wall and starts swiping open keyboards and touch screens. Soon, the white balcony-like space booms with Doctor Baldwin's voice. Laura remembers the man well, though he's always worked more closely with Dennis Jenkins than Laura herself.

"I've told you several times," the man says while facing Bill and Maria. "The risk is always there. But if the information Doctor Solomon sent us is true, you are just as safe as your Chipped friends would have been during the operation."

A gasp escapes Luna's lips. Laura frowns but doesn't join in Luna's dramatic and utterly boring human behavior. *Huh*, she thinks to herself. *Jenkins is dead?*

"And the information says what?" Bill's hands gesture wildly. "And in English, please. None of that medical nonsense this time."

Baldwin looks at Maria, his eyes pleading. Though Laura knows Baldwin used to be William's therapist, he's now looking at Maria for backup. The rebel leader can be a handful. That's what Jenkins always says. *What Dennis used to say*, Laura corrects herself. She swallows and allows the nagging, bothersome feeling to wash over her. But only for a nanosecond.

"Oh, don't look at me," Maria says and nods at Bill. "I'm with him. Spit it out, Baldwin. And explain it in a way that we all understand. Even Sanna."

One step back toward the wall. That's all Laura allows herself when she hears the familiar name. Her daughter's name. The nagging feeling washes through her again.

"The HSP research is incomplete. Statistical inference of incomplete data aside, there's the question of frequency, or multiple frequencies—"

Bill's brief scream cuts through the doctor's words. He paces away, toward what looks like a kitchen area, leaving Maria alone with the doctor.

"Okay Baldwin, you're doing it again." Maria nods at Sanna, hugging Kaarina in the corner of the room, both crying silently. "Remember? Like you'd explain it to *her*. Not me."

Baldwin gives Maria a half-smile. He walks to the operating table and looks around the flustered and broken crew of Unchipped refugees. "You are different, yes. And you are all hypersensitive, operating on a frequency and energy level that are simply unknown. Nurse Saarinen's research on HSP did lead her to an interdisciplinary challenge . . ."

When Maria clears her throat, the doctor stops to rephrase his words.

"Nurse Saarinen's research led her to a door." Baldwin raises his eyebrows at Maria. As she nods, he continues, "A door that should have brought her to the answer. What makes the Unchipped . . . Unchipped?"

"And?" Bill's high-pitched voice pierces from the kitchen.

"And once she opened that door, three new doors opened. Behind those doors—more doors. Each door represents a question. All of these doors are questions that need more research. Once she was done with those, six more doors opened behind each and every one of them. More data needed. More questions. More—"

"So you still don't know shit. Is that what you're saying, *doctor*?"

Laura tries to remember the name of the man who looks like a Hispanic catalog model, but stops bothering after a few seconds.

"Nobody knows, Micky," Owena says. Her voice has a strange innocence to it. Her face is too round, and her eyes too full of knowledge for her age. "That's what the doctor is saying. Nobody knows."

Baldwin stares at the ninja-girl, a quizzical look on his face. His interest in this woman is obvious. Almost obsessive. And it's clearly professional interest.

Why?

Laura closes her eyes and enters the database that is her mind. She accesses a database back in City of Finland, and scans through Nurse Saarinen's notes on the mind remapping project.

Nothing.

She keeps scanning. HSP. Singularity. Nanotech. Picobots.

Nothing.

Then, a lonely file, stored by Nurse Saarinen on the CS in City of Finland. But the file is not stored in one of Nurse Saarinen's devices, but on a private computer, which only one person has access to. Or only one person *should* have access to. Laura Solomon. Nurse Saarinen has saved her top-secret research right under Laura's nose—the one place where Laura hasn't bothered to look—on her own personal computer.

TEST SUBJECT 0 - OWENA

While Baldwin keeps explaining about the dechipping operation allegedly being safe for the Unchipped,

Laura learns about the secret project Nurse Saarinen's been running for years. During those years, Laura was still down there, running City of Finland—running the world. Back then, she would scan every single folder and file that was ever uploaded into the CS. Every employee file, every document ever created. Anything that took place in the AR and beyond. Everything, except for one computer.

Her own.

"That slippery little viper."

Her half-whisper gets Luna's attention. Her eyes are bewildered by the rush of emotion.

"What are you looking at, mouth breather?"

Too stunned to answer Laura's mocking question, Luna just shakes her head. Then she turns back to the scene in the mansion.

A broad man with a sharp face steps in front of the screen, blocking the view completely. "The only way past those drones is a chip-free brain." The mountain of a man steps closer to the operating table and picks up one of the chipping helmets. It takes Laura a moment to remember who he is. "I'll go first. Test it. If I don't make it, you'll have your answer."

A loud chatter fills the room. Luna shakes her head, wiping her forehead of sweat that isn't really there. Laura rolls her eyes and investigates her white coat. She almost wishes for a piece of lint or a stain. Something she could get rid of.

"What can we do?" Luna says, still staring at her friends. "Laura, we must do something. If the drones have located Dennis and Markus . . . Holy fuck, then Nurse Saarinen must have realized they went to the mansion after all."

Laura nods and gives Luna a sad smile.

"Don't just stand there nodding, Laura, she knows where they are. She can get to Sanna."

Two seconds. That's how long it takes Laura this time to remember her daughter's name. While communicating with Luna, half of her brain has kept scanning the fascinating cloning research Nurse Saarinen has carried out. Why did she keep this from Laura? Just something to have in her back pocket? It's like she's in between two forces, pulling her in opposite directions. The void. Nurse Saarinen's mind cloning project. She wants to jump into both.

"Laura, I swear . . . "

"Jenkins has an assistant."

Luna blinks at her. "What?"

"Starts with an H." Solomon frowns. "Maybe J."

Closing her eyes, Luna takes a deep breath. Her closed fists have started to shake. "Jenny."

Solomon snaps her fingers. "That's what it's called, yes."

A loud huff. Luna stares at Laura in disbelief. "*It?*"

"Him. Her. *Hän.* Doesn't matter. Search for her AR-glasses from the database and call her. She'll be with those little worker ants . . ." Laura's fingers snap repeatedly, her focus torn between Luna, the mansion, the clone, and the luring void.

"The CFU?"

"*Juuri se.*"

"Laura, I don't speak a word of Finnish. You know this."

"Mm."

Luna spreads her arms and turns to take a breather. Laura does the same, using the moment to walk back to the void. She takes yet another peek down.

While staring into the only place in the universe where she doesn't have access—while her mind keeps educating itself on Nurse Saarinen's cloning research— Laura hears Luna speaking rapidly to someone over a set of AR-glasses.

Why is she wearing glasses here? She doesn't need . . .

The pull gets stronger. The black hole beneath draws her to sit down on the edge. The white glow, her daughter's name, Luna's moods . . . it all fades away.

All that remains is a black nothing.

" . . . and I can't find Jenny, but this woman called Celine, and a guy called Dylan stepped up. She's a cook from City of Maine, says she knew Margaret. They've hacked into the troops leaving City of California, disabling their vehicles. But this only buys us two or three hours."

Luna's words sound as though they're coming from under water. Still staring into the void, Laura hums a tune, oblivious to the sense of urgency in Luna's voice. The song reminds her of her mother, but she can't quite recall why.

"Christmas jingles?" Luna grunts loudly. "Could you *please* just snap out of this psycho mode of yours? Baldwin wants to talk to you about recovery time."

Christmas Eve. Ham with a thick layer of mustard cooking in the oven. Fresh pine needles landing on a red, round carpet. With the determination only a ten-year-old girl can have, Laura has been demanding the tree for weeks. Now, the tree is half-stripped of its needles. Soon it'll be tossed out, having fulfilled its brief purpose. It'll rot in the compost area between the playhouse and garage.

"Laura? Laura! Don't make me throw the other shoe—"

"It's time for your boyfriend to come out, dear."

Blinking, Luna makes a strange sound. Stunned, unsure what to do or say, she twitches and blinks, like *she's* the robot, and not Owena's clone at the mansion.

"Jovan, right?" Laura gives Luna a motherly smile. Fake, but motherly nonetheless. "He's cooked in there long enough. Don't you think? Go inside, contact Iris, and let him out. Ef will take care of the rest."

Breathing sharply, Luna turns to look at the see-through screen, showing the scene that is the mansion. Then she looks at the doorway that leads back into the white glow, and away from the balcony.

"Well go on. You know what to do."

Doubt, rage, and joy take turns on Luna's face.

"Who knows, maybe he wants to upload?" Laura nods at the door, her lips pressing into a stern smile. "One way to find out."

"I know you're playing with me," Luna says but side-steps toward the white glow. The thought of releasing her boyfriend from the stasis capsule pulls her, just like the void pulls Laura.

"And what's my end game? Hmm?" When Luna bites her lower lip and doesn't reply, Laura contin-ues, "To have someone else here with you, perhaps? Someone to keep you company so I can work in peace?"

After closing her eyes, Luna half-whispers, "And the mansion?"

"Let me take care of the mansion, dear. Like you said, my daughter . . . *Sanna* is there. I'm going to help them."

"You're going to let Sanna dechip? Even after Nurse Saarinen's inadequate research data?"

Never. Never in a million years.

Laura shrugs. "Seems like the only way out."

After Luna steps into the white glow, Laura turns to tap the wall. After a few swipes, the AR-glasses on Doctor Baldwin's chest pocket buzz to life. She watches as the man steps away from his heated conversation with Bill and Maria. He sets the glasses on his face and steps over to the spiral staircase for privacy.

"Doctor Solomon. How nice of you to join us."

"I need you to find the girl," she says, not bothering with small talk. That part of her human personality—her hatred for redundant chitchat—is still going strong.

"Your daughter?"

"Yes, Samantha." Laura shakes her head and forces her mind to focus. "Sammy. I mean, Sanna. Get Sanna on the phone."

"Phone?" Doctor Baldwin hesitates. "Doctor Solomon, we haven't used phones since The Great Affliction—"

"You know what I mean," Laura snaps.

"My apologies," Baldwin says slowly while walking upstairs. "I will get your daughter, but doctor, the AR-glasses will cause her tremendous pain."

"She's not down there with you?" Laura's brow rises. "Why?"

"She's upstairs with Owena and her pet rabbit. We figured it's better for them to focus on playing. They both seem to be in shock."

The clone is not in shock, Laura thinks but doesn't say it out loud. *The clone just doesn't care.*

"Doctor Solomon?"

"Mm?"

"The AR-glasses will hurt the girl—"

"Then you interpret the conversation. Just tell her I need to speak with her."

Without even noticing, Laura has opened a new file in Nurse Saarinen's cloning research. She scans the pages, downloading more information while she waits for Baldwin to walk upstairs.

Two girls stare at the man wearing AR-glasses. The younger one—or seemingly younger one, the file says Owena is only five years old—covers her eyes and crawls to a corner.

Baldwin turns around to face away from Sanna. "It's worse this time. She's been away from Chip-technology for too long. I don't think I can be in the same room with her while we have the conversation."

"How about the other girl?"

"Owena?"

"Yes. She's Chipped, right? She can take the call."

After pausing for a moment, Baldwin gestures for Owena to come to the door. He hands the AR-glasses to the girl-woman, and whispers something in her ear. With a serious look on her face, the clone nods at Baldwin. She puts the glasses on.

"Owena?" Laura says, surprised to hear her own voice shake slightly. Curiosity. Another trace of humanity that remains in her, sticky and strong.

"Yes. And you are Doctor Solomon."

"I am."

Laura peeks over her shoulder. Luna must be busy with releasing her boyfriend from his capsule prison. She peeks over Owena's shoulder. Baldwin has vanished too, probably back downstairs to continue preparing the operations. It's just Laura and the girls now.

"You want me to talk to Sanna."

"Actually, dear. It's you I wanted to talk to."

"Me?" The clone tilts her head, a slight tic taking over her right eyebrow.

Well done, Nurse Saarinen.

"Yes, Owena. You. I need a favor. Something I would like to try. Sort of a magic trick."

"What's magic?"

"Never mind that, dear. Let's play a game."

The clone nods, a satisfied look on her face. "I know games. I'm good at them."

"Good." Laura smiles, excitement washing through her. The void pulling her toward the edge loosens its grip on her a little bit.

And now I get to play with your shiniest, newest toy.

"How does this game start?"

"Well, dear . . . Do you see that balcony railing behind you?"

A nod.

"I want you to climb over the railing, jump down, and run to the guard's shed by the gates."

The clone slips into the small guard's shed by the rusty mansion gates. Zigzagging between the cardboard boxes and hundreds of cigarette butts, Owena makes her way to a metal closet at the back of the room. She opens the cabinet and waits for Laura's instructions.

"Pick your poison, dear."

"Poison?" A robotic head tilt. "All I see is weapons."

"Mm." Laura suppresses her chuckle. *Nice job, old friend. This little pet of yours is a real gem.*

"My bad, dear. Poor choice of words. Pick your *weapon*. You need something you're familiar with. Something easy to aim."

One by one, the clone starts pulling the weapons out of the closet. Laura frowns, confused about what's going on.

"What's going on, dear?"

"You said to pick the ones I'm familiar with."

"I did . . . "

"I'm familiar with all of these. They're all easy to aim."

This time, Laura can't muffle her laugh. *Added some entertainment value, did we?*

"Let me rephrase that, dear. Pick the one that is the best for shooting down small objects in the night sky."

"Objects?"

"Drones."

Without stopping to think about it, Owena lets most of the weapons drop to the floor. A target rifle in her hands, she leaves the guard's shed and marches toward the front yard. The mansion door remains shut. The drone still hovers above a lifeless body on the gravel, waiting.

"I just shoot it down?"

"Mhm. Yes dear."

The clone stops where the brown grass ends and the gravel begins. As she aims the gun at the drone, the buzzing device rotates in place, seemingly staring straight at Owena. Will it kill one of its own? Can it fire at objects on the ground or just hack them?

Owena's gun fires silently. The bullet passes right through the center of the drone, barely shaking it. It hovers in the air for a fraction of a second more before dropping to the earth like a stone.

"Is that all you needed, Doctor Sol—"

The rifle drops onto the long grass. The girl's head bows and her whole body seems to have frozen solid.

"Dear? Uh . . ." What the hell did Nurse Saarinen name this thing again. "Owena?"

In the distance, the drone beeps once, twice, three times on the ground before its red light dies. The girl looks at the drone, then looks at the weapon on the ground and starts to kneel down to get it.

"Who is this, please?" The nasal voice coming from Owena is not hers. It's someone else speaking to Laura through the clone. Laura takes a sharp breath in, then chuckles, and shakes her head.

"Well, well, well. I didn't know this was a multi-player game, dear nurse."

The clone freezes and seems to forget about the rifle on the ground. She stands back up and stares into space.

"La . . . *Laura?*"

Stepping onto the glowing white wall, Laura taps on the monitor camera to see what's going on inside the mansion. The girl—her girl—is now downstairs with the other mortals.

Laura mutes the clone's AR-glasses. Nurse Saarinen hasn't said another word. When Laura doesn't reply to her, the clone starts marching forward.

Nurse Saarinen has recovered enough to continue operating Owena, after learning her old colleague and employer is still alive.

Somewhat alive.

But if the clone walks into the mansion, this might not be the case for Laura's daughter and the rest of the mortals. They'd surely all be dead in the matter of a few minutes.

Nurse Saarinen scans the yard and mansion through Owena's eyes until her gaze fixes on Baldwin's car and the cables connected to it. "So that's how you got past the Faraday cage," she says. "Clever." The clone starts marching toward the mansion.

"Novak!" Laura calls for Luna while opening new screens on the wall. Only a few seconds later, Luna's head peeks in from the white glow.

"Which of these clowns knows how to fight?"

"Clowns? What?"

"No time to be confused," Laura says with a calm voice. "Point at the mortals who could potentially fight a killer clone. It's a long shot, but there's not much more we can do for them."

Luna runs to the screens and sees Owena opening the mansion's front door. "Is she—"

"Yup. Nurse Saarinen. But she dropped her gun, so it's going to be a fistfight. Focus on the task at hand, Novak."

"Maria."

Laura taps the speaker open for Luna. "Maria, ten o'clock. It's not, um . . . " Luna's lost for words, panicking, "It's not Owena who's about to walk in. It's Nurse Saarinen."

On the screen, Maria looks around the ceiling, spinning around once, then staring at the door, her muscles tensed and ready to attack.

"Okay, so chica can fight," Laura says. "Who else?"

Luna shakes her head. "That's it."

Laura turns to stare at her in disbelief. "What?"

"Just Maria. She's ex combat something-something. No one else has gone through any training. Not that I'm aware of anyway. I mean, Yeti is a rock, but I've never seen him fight with anyone."

"Unbelievable . . . " Laura mutters. She swipes open another screen in front of Luna and points at the group of people on the monitor screen. "Give that one mixed martial art skills. The chip number is in his file. You know what name to search."

"But he's Unchipped—"

"You're way behind, Novak. Yes, he's Unchipped. Yes, I haven't been able to hack into their brain before. Yes, I now have access, thanks to Nurse Saarinen's research." Laura swipes the air and types in numbers to a hovering screen above them. "Just add this code snippet at the end of the command."

"Okay . . . " Luna opens her screen, then shakes her head in confusion. "Sorry, whose chip am I hacking?"

Laura makes a circling gesture at the screen that shows the mansion. "That one."

Now it's Luna's time to stare at Laura. "Bill? You want to make *Bill* a warrior?"

"No time to argue. Not if you want to save your friends."

Owena opens the mansion's door and steps inside. Baldwin and the rest of the mortals back away into the corner behind the monitor and other operating machines. Maria takes a step closer to the clone. For a long time, the two of them just stare at each other.

"Is it done? The MMA download?" Laura asks Luna, coolness in her voice.

Luna's fingers move fast on the see-through keyboard. "In a minute . . . but Laura, this isn't going to work. He's Unchipped . . . "

"I said, don't worry about that. Just do it and do it quickly."

Half a minute goes by. Maria and the clone are slowly creeping closer to one another. Time seems to have stopped in the mansion. Nurse Saarinen is putting on a show. Enjoying this, instead of getting it done.

"Download completed," Luna says, staring at the screen, then at Laura, then back at the screen with wide eyes.

Laura taps a glowing microphone icon. Then mutes it again and turns to look at Luna. "What's his name again?"

"Fucking William!"

The microphone taps on again. "William, go close that door before more drones arrive. And help Marisa to fight this—"

"Maria!" Luna cries. "Her name is Maria."

Bill looks around the room, reluctant to step forward.

Luna shoves Laura aside and taps the microphone. "Bill, just do it. I just gave you full-on ninja powers. You're now just as badass as Maria is."

"What?" His high-pitched voice makes Laura's head jerk back a bit. She gestures Luna to move aside and takes over the microphone again.

"Congratulations, your chip has been upgraded. Now go close the door."

Luna taps the floor nervously. "What if he doesn't believe us—"

A loud scream startles them both. Bill leaps through the air, past Maria, past the waiting clone, all the way to the mansion door. The door slams shut, and everyone freezes. Bill lands on one knee, then looks up at the clone with bewildered eyes.

"Jesus . . . " someone says from the corner of the room.

". . . on a bike," another mortal ends the sentence.

Nurse Saarinen's clone attacks Maria, who slips under the strike. Another scream echoes in the mansion hallway as Bill runs and leaps again to help his friend.

"I guess he believed us," Laura says to Luna.

"Looks like."

The clone swings at Maria, who blocks the strike, then turns and kicks at Bill, who staggers back. Maria turns and kicks at the woman's kneecaps but lowers her hands a little and takes a kick to the temple that sends her reeling. Bill grabs Owena from behind and pulls her down, trying to get an arm around her neck for a chokehold. But the clone is too strong. She wriggles free of the chokehold and nearly gets his arm in an armbar before he manages to escape. Then Owena bounces back onto her feet, throwing Bill sideways and charging at Maria again.

Sighing deeply, Laura walks off, heading to the edge. She folds her hands behind her back and looks down at the void. Its call is strong again, the pull tighter around her mind.

"Can't we just make them all badass warriors?" Luna rushes after her, just to fast-walk back to the screen where the fight is taking place.

"Sure," Laura hollers, her back turned to Luna. "How many of your little friends are you willing to risk?"

"*Risk*?"

"William's chip didn't rupture during the MMA download. But it certainly might have."

"And you're telling me this *now*?!" Luna's voice is high-pitched. "What kind of a chance?"

"I'd say fifty-fifty."

Funny how easy it is to see Luna's human and computer sides fighting one another. *Mortals,* Laura thinks. *How boring.*

Though Laura must admit, it's impressive that she's already able to activate her rational side, even though her training has barely begun.

"Well?" Laura says, staring at Luna. "Who's it going to be?"

"I don't know. I don't want to risk anybody . . . " Luna buries her face in her hands. "Yeti, let's do Yeti! He's strong as fuck. He'll make it!"

"No, I don't want to mess with that one's chip," Laura says, remembering the day the big man—apparently named *Yeti* of all ridiculous names mortals come up with—was chipped in City of Finland.

"What? Why not?"

"The conversion rate might be poor. His brain is not stable. The training file might not take."

"Because he's Unchipped? But Bill is too."

"Not because of that, but because of his past. Scan his medical history. You'll see."

"Laura, that shit is private."

"You've already looked up William's file. How is this . . . *Yeti* different?"

"Looking up a chip number to give Bill powers is one thing. Besides, I already know Bill's medical history. Everyone does. He's very open about it these days. In his head, I mean." Luna waves her hands in the air, flustered and unfocused. "The tapping thing we do."

"I'm aware of the concept. What does that have to do with looking up the Finnish man's file?"

"Yeti doesn't do that," Luna says, pacing on a small spot by the screen. She stops to take a glance at the screen and then continues her pace. The fight must be going well for her allies. "He barely ever lets anyone inside his mind. Going through his personal information . . . Yeah, no. I can't do that."

Leaning closer to the edge, gaping at the blackness beneath her, Laura sighs. "Suit yourself. Two warriors against one it is."

Luna continues to stare at the fight, but Laura doesn't bother. She can tell what's going on just by the grunts and cries Luna lets out. When she starts a mantra of curse words in her native Serbian, Laura rolls her eyes and turns to face her.

"Okay, Novak. Time to think more like a computer and less like a train-wreck. We have no use for your outrage and worry. If you think we need another fighter, just point one out. If not, be quiet and wait it out. You're driving me insane with all that huffing and puffing."

"But the risk . . ."

"I'm telling you. Dechipping, downloading, uploading . . . Yes, there's a risk, but it's way less significant than what I've thought. Nurse Saarinen's research wasn't all useless, you know."

She watches Luna take deep breaths. *Why? Why does she still have the need to do that?*

After a long exhale, a neutral expression on her face, Luna asks, "So you'll let Sanna dechip?"

"If she doesn't upload, yes."

"And what exactly did you learn?"

"About what?"

"About the Unchipped brain," Luna says, her voice shaking but under control.

"Bits and pieces. Enough to know how to get in and out of the Unchipped mind. It's still all there, just not activated at the same frequency as a properly chipped brain is. Your people vibrate at a different energy level. That's why the sonic weapon affects them but not those who are properly chipped. Just like the weapon, once I find that level, I can access the chip, no problem."

"This is the same frequency Nurse Saarinen used to put me down in United Inland?"

"The very same. I'm just using it to access a brain, not to destroy it. It's a lot like Bill being bipolar. The way his mind works has nothing to with his strengths or weaknesses. It's just a different formula of the same bits and pieces. Neither Eastern nor Western medicine has ever truly understood the mind, only small fractions of it."

"And why is Yeti so different?"

"Gamma-aminobutyric acid."

Confusion visits Luna's seemingly calm face. After pausing, she sighs and spreads her hands at Laura.

Laura waves her off. "A story for another time."

Frowning, Luna turns toward the wall to focus on the task at hand. "He's too busy to fight anyway." Laura glances at the screen and sees the big man holding a hysterically crying woman at the corner of the room. Laura sighs, stands still, hands folded behind her white lab coat, her mind traveling back in time.

Fish eggs.

Potato, carrot, liver, and rutabaga casserole.

Silver candlesticks lighting the Christmas dinner she wants nothing to do with. She's not hungry. Not one bit. Not when at least fifteen gifts are waiting under the tree with her name on them. But she also knows the rule: no opening the presents until her plate's empty. Stacking peas on her fork, she stares at the largest present under the tree, wrapped in white gift paper . . .

"This fight is not fair!" Luna cries out, distracting Laura from her thoughts. "Look!"

"The robot is winning because it's not attached to its emotions."

"But Maria and Bill are humans. They can't do that."

"You really think humans can't detach from their feelings?" Laura's head jerks back in surprise. "Huh."

When Luna blinks at her, unsure how to respond, Laura gives in and walks away from the edge. Once she's next to Luna, she sighs and joins her, staring at the screen.

Owena is circling Bill and Maria without engaging. Bill keeps throwing short little jabs to keep her from rushing in, while Maria bounces on the balls of her feet, her eyes locked with Owena's. Finally, the clone attacks. She launches at Bill who blocks her. Owena strikes again, head butting him and breaking his nose. She executes a quick combination that drops Bill to the floor, then turns and punches Maria in the throat just in time. The woman gasps in stunned pain, stepping back with both hands at her neck.

Owena turns back to Bill just as he's struggling to his feet. He attempts an elbow strike but she easily dodges it, then knocks him down again with a rapid series of strikes. Just as Laura sighs, about to return to stare at the void and her childhood memories, Maria charges at Owena and drives a fist into her lower back then kicks at her kidneys. Owena winces in agony and staggers away from Bill. Maria grabs the wounded Bill and pulls him to the side. She lets go of him just in time to block Owena's newest attack.

"I can't watch this." Luna turns away from the screen. "This is killing me."

Laura stares at the fight on the screen. For the longest time, the two women punch and kick at each other, both of them refusing to give in.

Finally, Bill manages to get back on his feet again. Another scream fills the mansion as he charges at Owena—just to lose balance and fall back to the floor. Before Owena has time to turn and refocus on Maria, Maria's foot lands under Owena's chin. The kick throws her off balance and she falls to the floor, hitting her head hard against the white marble. Maria climbs on top of her, pins her down, and slams her head into the marble once, twice, three times. A silence falls over the mansion.

"You can look now, Novak," Laura says, her voice neutral. "I think they're finally done."

Laura's words snap Luna out of her confusion. She looks back at the screen. Owena lies on the floor, Maria, Bill, and the Yeti-mortal pinning her down. Doctor Baldwin hurries over with a square cage gadget. They place the cage on the clone's head.

"We need to dechip her," one of the mortals says. "And we need to do it fast."

A panicky chatter fills the room. People argue, some crying, some yelling at each other, and seemingly to no one in particular.

"How long do we have until the troops arrive?"

"I'd say three hours. Maybe more," Baldwin's voice booms in the room. "It's hard to say how long it'll take them to realize the CFU has hijacked their vehicles. But they'll send more for sure."

"And how long to recover from the operation?" Maria asks, nodding at the stack of chipping helmets.

"If all goes well," Baldwin pauses to think, "An hour, maybe two. But you will be nauseated and weak."

"But we can pass the drones," Kaarina says, her arms around Sanna. "Disappear into the desert. Rest somewhere out of sight."

"Technically, yes. But . . . "

"Then let's do this," Yeti says, getting up from the floor where the clone lies frozen, seemingly turned off. "Let's dechip and get the fuck out of here."

Baldwin looks around the room. "We only have two operating tables."

"So we lie on the floor," the catalog model says, pressing himself quickly against Bill, whispering something in his ear. A question. Worry shadows his face. When Bill nods, the man rushes up the stairs. "I'll get us blankets and pillows so we can set it up."

Letting her mind slip, Laura dives back into the mind mapping research. The more data she devours, the more pressing her urge to call Nurse Saarinen and talk shop. How had she missed all of this? How did the nurse manage to keep research this significant from Laura? Why would she?

She's always known her colleague—her right-hand woman—to be a mastermind. A one-of-a-kind scientist who never bothered to update a title that was way below her know-how and education. Modest and hyperbolical at the same time. Nurse Saarinen and Doctor Solomon. Together, they had conquered the world. Become the sole leaders of a new society, a new government. Imagine the things they could do *now*, with the ability to clone people's minds, hack anyone's chips, while having unlimited access . . .

"Hey, doc!" Luna's shoe lands next to Laura, just at the edge of the void, then falls silently down into it. "It's about to start. Baldwin has everyone ready to go."

Already?

"Quit staring into that black thing and come supervise this."

Not moving a muscle, Laura reluctantly exits the mind mapping files and refocuses on Luna's voice. The mansion, the dechipping, the mortals . . . after the latest data dump, it all can be described with one single word.

Boring.

"Doctor Solomon?" Baldwin's voice echoes around Laura. Standing perfectly still, her eyes still scanning the nothingness beneath, Laura replies, "What is it you need, Doctor?"

"I'm running low on sedatives."

"And?"

"And I need you to locate more."

A feeling of someone staring her down makes Laura finally turn around and face the wall. Luna's furious expression causes Laura to stop for half a second. She raises her eyebrows at her wannabe colleague. *What's your problem*? Laura thinks to herself, knowing she doesn't need to be Unchipped for Luna to read her mind.

"It's like you don't care at all."

"It's like you haven't heard a word about detaching your emotions from your work."

"It's your daughter."

The kid. Sanna. Right. For a moment there, Laura forgot the girl even existed.

Her finger taps the microphone icon. "I can't do proper anesthesia from here, but I can make them more comfortable during the dechipping."

"Please do." The doctor stands in the middle of a floor, surrounded by seven nervously twitching people. Sanna lies between Kaarina and the catalog-man, holding their hands. Tears stream down her face, but Laura can't hear the sobs. Something moves within her, an unsettling feeling.

"Is she that scared of the helmet?" Laura asks, half-whispering.

"Are you serious?" Luna asks. "She just lost two people that are practically family to her."

"Who, now?"

"Dennis and Markus!"

Laura tilts her head, keeping her gaze on the girl. "But Jenkins and the boy were Chipped. They couldn't have been that close."

Shaking her head, Luna stares at Laura. "Unbelievable."

"What?"

"You are so out of touch, and it's beyond this place and death and whatever else has happened to you over the last year. Honestly, I'm speechless."

Laura shrugs a shoulder. The fact that the Chipped and Unchipped strangers can care for each other on an emotional level makes this tiresome event a tad more interesting.

"Novak, download the nitrous oxide simulation nanobot instructions to all of their chips. For the clone, give a triple dose."

Blink, blink. Fingers hovering above her see-through keyboard, Luna stares at Laura puzzled. "Nitrous what now?"

"Laughing gas. The bots will work the same way as nitrous does, releasing dopamine and stimulating the mesolimbic reward pathway in the brain."

Blink. "Of course they will."

"Just do it, Novak."

Looking for lint, Laura picks at her lab coat, straightening the sleeves. She's tempted to see what would happen if she manipulated her own sense of time. Fast-forwarding to the moment when the mortals are chip-free and roaming in the wilderness like a group of drunken apes. Maybe then, she could contact Nurse Saarinen and pick her brain about the clone. How many more Owenas exist? Could Laura download herself into a clone to visit Nurse Saarinen?

The thought tempts Laura more than anything else at the moment. To see the genius nurse's secret research lab in City of Spain. To be able to hop from one mortal to another, controlling them . . .

Three thumps against her back wake Laura from her daydreaming. No, not dreams. Her *plans*. Because gods don't dream, they create . . .

Laura's suddenly struck by a rapid-fire of shoes. Some of the shoes land on the floor, some fall silently over the edge and disappear into the void.

"Hey, doc!" Luna yells. "Come. *On*."

Laura turns around and glares at Luna. "Your anger issues are more tiresome than this dechipping nonsense."

On the screen, seven mortals lie on the floor— laughing, giggling, and chuckling. *Drunken apes.* Chipping helmets attached to their heads, they lie on white blankets and sheets.

"This setup is a joke," she mumbles.

"Is it not safe?" Luna hurries to ask. "I thought with the chipping helmets there isn't a risk of infection or error . . . "

"There's always a risk," Laura says.

"They want to be free."

Laura scoffs. "Free to eat rat meat and weeds for the rest of their lives? Like those hippies up at the vineyard?"

"What hippies?"

A wave of her hand. "Just forget it."

"You know, if you showed some common decency, you could actually help."

"I gave them laughing gas. Didn't I?"

"No, *I* gave them laughing gas. All you've done is bark commands and zone off to stare at that doom hole, over and over and over again."

"It's part of your training. You've got it under control. Once you figure out the code, I don't have to waste any more of my time on it. And you seem to have your panties in a twist every time something minor happens down there. So there. You take over, I'll move on to other things. It's a win-win."

"Un-fucking-believable."

"What? What else do you need from me?"

"You haven't said one word to Sanna. Not one syllable to comfort her. You've not shown any support to Doctor Baldwin, assisted him in any way . . ."

"I'm sorry," Laura says and laughs briefly. "*Assisted*? I haven't been an assistant to anyone in my life, and I'm not about to start now. I'm more powerful than all of the mortals' processing power combined."

"You did not just call your own daughter a mortal. Like she's some low-level bug in the system."

My system.

"Novak, you need to . . . "

"Tell me to detach myself from my feelings one more time." Luna's voice is unnaturally calm. She tries on a smile. "Go on, do it."

A deep breath in. It happens before Laura can stop it. A reflex. A need. *How disappointingly human of me.*

The side of Laura's mouth twitches into a half-second smile. "Fine."

Luna stares at her. "Fine, what?"

"I'll talk to her. Them. I'll talk, and I'll see if Doctor Baldwin needs any … " Laura stops to clear her throat. Another remnant of human behavior has returned. "I'll see if he needs any *advice* from me. Okay?"

After stepping away from the wall, Luna gestures at the keyboard in front of her, exaggerating her enthusiasm. "Please. Don't mind me."

"But I do."

"Do what?" Luna asks.

"Mind you being here." Before she can stop herself, Laura shifts her weight from one foot to another. Gods don't get nervous. Do they? "How about you give me some privacy?"

"Fine, Laura. I'll leave. But you better follow through, or else … "

"Or else you'll switch to high heels?"

Shaking her head, Luna disappears back inside. Alone on the glowing white ledge, Laura stares at the group of people on the floor and the doctor hovering nearby. Her finger on the microphone icon, she clears her throat.

"Doctor . . ." She clears her throat again. "Robert?"

He stops by the monitor. Hands filled with wires, Doctor Baldwin looks up, his face overwhelmed and tired. "Yes, Doctor Solomon."

"Please, dear. Call me Laura."

A breath escapes Baldwin's lips. "Of course. Laura."

Laura opens her mouth to talk, but suddenly she has no words. How is she supposed to help this man? Or comfort the girl? That's not what she does. Her job has always been hands-on, not emotional support. Isn't calling people "dear" and "sweetheart" enough?

"How is it going down there?" She tucks her chin and shakes her head at her own words. She's terrible at this.

"Well underway. I'm just worried about complications. The reverse method isn't really something I've ever done before."

"No one has."

"Yeah, no . . . " The doctor spreads his arms and chuckles. "Precisely."

He seems . . . worried. Anxious. *Human.*

"Hey, don't be so . . . You are . . . " Laura rubs the bridge of her nose. Doing great? Doing a great job? The best you can? "You're doing your hardest. I mean your best self."

Oh, for the love of . . .

"I'm sorry?"

"Great. You're doing great, and the best you can in a highly uncommon situation."

Laura steps back and spins around in frustration. This is not what she does. This is what Novak is for. Words. Consoling. All that emotional crap.

"Thank you for that, Doctor. *Laura.*" Baldwin's expression has changed. He's stopped fidgeting. Stopped spinning around, checking the same wire and helmet for the eleventh time. "Means a lot, coming from you. I feel much more confident when I have you supervising this."

"No, hey. I'm just here to assist. That's all. You've already done all the work."

His smile moves something within Laura's mind. Not an unsettling feeling this time, but something else. Something . . . warm.

"Well, they've all gone under. The rest is up to the helmets. Is there a way to know how far along the process is?"

Laura frowns. "You're asking me?"

"Well . . . yeah. You can access any computer, right?" Baldwin walks over to Sanna, and kneels to read some small print on the side of her chipping helmet. The girl seems to be asleep, her face cleared of worry but still damp with tears. "Try checking this one." He runs his finger on a small metal label on the side of the helmet. "CA-two-four-three-four-two-five-eight."

Laura stares, her mind entering the numbers into a black screen. The cursor blinks twice, and a snippet of code appears. Laura reads the code. Then rereads it, blinks, and reads it again. An uneasy feeling washes through her. The emotions shake her body in a way she didn't know was still possible.

"Robert, they're dying."

The man blinks rapidly, staring into space. "What?"

"Removing an object from the cortex created a chemical reaction that I've never seen happen before. The nanobots are destroying not just themselves but their host as well."

Baldwin stands up straight, a frightful look on his face while he stares at his patients on the floor. He moves sideways to another chipping helmet and reads the number on its side. Laura taps the numbers in, though she already knows what the computer will tell her.

"He is dying too."

Baldwin runs to another patient, frantically calling out numbers. Laura sighs and enters the numbers in.

"She's dying as well. Robert, they're all dying."

He stands up and holds his hand, then cups his hands on his mouth and murmurs, "The data collection . . ."

"Yup," Laura says listlessly, looking for lint on her lab coat. "Not enough memory space." *I told you so,* Laura thinks but doesn't bother saying it out loud. What's the use? She has nothing to prove to anyone. A lion doesn't have to tell a bunch of kittens that she's a lion.

"How can we make it stop?"

"We can't."

Laura watches Baldwin in silence as the doctor slowly processes the fact that all his patients are about to die. While he circles around them, aimlessly checking wires and then stopping to hold on to his head, a shade from the staircase makes its way over.

A rabbit.

Laura tilts her head and watches the rodent hop over to her daughter. "Hm . . . " She opens the City of Finland's database and hacks into the old lab reports. Her eyes scan the reports. "Just as I thought," she mumbles.

"What did you say, Laura?" Baldwin turns his gaze up toward the ceiling. "Help me fix this, please. I can't just stand here and watch them die."

"You might not have to," Laura says, her voice calm and collected. "Robert, I need you to focus. Can you do that for me?"

His eyes are bewildered, but the man nods.

Laura nods too. "Good. See that rabbit? Climbing on Samantha's lap?" She closes her eyes and curses her glitchy memory but doesn't bother to correct herself.

Baldwin looks around and then strides over to Sanna. "I see the rabbit. It must have hopped down from upstairs." He picks up the rabbit and wraps his arms around it like it's the most valuable and treasured being on the planet.

"Okay, listen carefully. When the rabbit was brought to City of Finland, it was chipped in the lab for testing purposes. I have the chip number and all the data here with me. I'm going to sedate the rabbit now, then upload it."

Baldwin's mouth opens, but not a word comes out. Laura taps on the controls and enters one code command after another. Once she's ready, she steps back, her finger hovering on the enter key.

"Ready?"

Baldwin looks down at the bunny and caresses its head. He nods.

Laura taps the enter key. The rabbit's head jerks back and then settles to rest lifeless against Baldwin's chest. From the corner of her eyes, Laura sees a glitching image. When she turns to look, a white-black bunny sits in the middle of the white glow, its paws spread as if to help it balance on an uneven surface.

"Huh."

"Laura … what …" Startled, Baldwin sets the dead rabbit on the floor and takes a hurried step back. "We killed the rabbit."

"Quite the opposite," Laura says and can't help but smile. She turns her back on Sanna's pet and starts tapping onto multiple screens on the wall, circling around them, opening databases, folders, and files.

"Okay, Robert," she says once the commands are ready to go. "Here's what we're going to … "

"Hold on." Baldwin's hand raises, gesturing for Laura to stop talking. Back in her human days, she'd be insulted by the interruption. Right now, she doesn't care. Instead of scolding Baldwin for being disrespectful, she stares at him in wonder. His nose is sniffing the air, his wide eyes scanning the mansion's windows.

So, he's definitely lost his mind. Maybe I should check his levels. Tweak his cerebellum activity …

"I smell smoke."

He races to the nearest window and peers outside. That's when Laura hears the intensifying buzz. Drones. A lot of them.

Baldwin runs to another window, this one facing at the side of the house where Dennis Jenkins lies dead. "No, no, no, no, no."

"What? What is it?" Laura's view is limited because of the monitor's angle.

"The barn is on fire again. It must have gotten a second wind. And the drones..." Baldwin disappears into the kitchen area, then after a moment, reappears by the monitor, staring straight into Laura's eyes.

"Laura, the drones are diving into the flames and spreading the sparks on the dead grass. The mansion's supports at the east end are now on fire." He takes off again, running to the other end of the hallway. He opens the pantry door and rushes in. There must be a window inside that small space. "The west side is in flames too. Laura, the drones are trapping us. They're going to burn us alive!"

"Either that," Laura mumbles to herself while tapping on her screen. "Or Nurse Saarinen will be sending missiles your way any moment now... "

"What?" Robert shrieks in panic.

"What? No, nothing. Just talking to myself."

Through her database, Laura scans through the statistics of past wildfires in California. She calculates the wind, the dryness, humidity, and temperature around the mansion, comparing the stats to the conditions at the moment.

Huh. That fast.

"You're right, Robert. You have about fifteen minutes before the mansion is fully engulfed."

Baldwin runs to the mortals on the floor. He kneels down next to Sanna, his hands nervously hovering over the blinking chipping helmet. "I can't carry them out of here, Laura! What are we going to do?"

Something soft pokes against Laura's ankle. As she looks down, Mr. Bun Bun stands on its hind legs and climbs against Laura's calf. "Huh . . . " She doesn't move, just stares at the creature and its rapidly wiggling nose. "Shoo, now."

"What? Laura, the smoke—"

"We're going to upload your patients. And I suggest . . . " Two more pokes against her ankle interrupt Laura. She leans down and picks up the bunny. "I suggest you join them, Robert."

He stands up, shaking his head, tears glimmering in his eyes. "The bunny." He swallows a panicky sob. "It survived?" Laura looks down at the critter lying against her arm. With her free hand, she briefly strokes the rabbit's head, momentarily lost in her blank mind.

"Laura?"

"Yes, Robert. The bunny is here. You can be too."

The man holds onto his head, a grimace stuck on his face.

"I'm afraid you're stuck in there too," Laura continues, fascinated by the man's dedication to his patients. "You still have your chip installed. The minute you're outside, the drones will identify you, and you'll share the same fate as Dennis Jenkins."

He looks up, desperation and panic on his face. "They'll hack me and blow up my chip."

"Indeed."

Baldwin stands up, staring at the end of the mansion. From the vents up on the walls, smoke snakes into the building. "So that's it. This is the end."

"Of your life on Earth?" Laura shrugs a shoulder. "Yes, Robert. That's it."

The man breaks down sobbing. On his knees, he buries his face in his palms, crying out loud as if he's already in tremendous pain.

What is this madness?

"Robert, it's okay. It's just one place and time. The end of an era."

He sobs on, words gurgling from his throat. "Nobody knows what happens when you die, Laura. I don't want to die. I don't believe in the afterlife."

Who in their right mind does? she thinks, but decides against saying that out loud.

With slow, short steps, Laura works her way around the wall. Her hand stroking the rabbit's back, she double-checks the screen. An assistant's job. Novak's job. That's what she's doing, but calling out for the girl would only cause more tiresome chaos and commotion. She's better off dealing with this part herself.

"Robert, it's time to go."

The man's sobs stop. His palms still pressed against his swollen eyes, Robert's whole body freezes. "What?"

"It's time. We have exactly six minutes and forty seconds to get you and your patients to safety."

Laura presses the enter keys, activating one code after another, command after command. Funny how programming used to be something she wasn't keen on doing. Something so elementary is far from fascinating, but in the end, it's not that different from tinkering with the human brain.

"I have patients one, two, four, and five ready to go. Are you easily nauseated, Robert?"

The doctor has hurried to the low stack of chipping helmets at the other operating table. He's putting on the helmet the Chipped man with overgrown hair was supposed to use—before Nurse Saarinen's drone fried his chip and his brain along with it.

"You don't need a helm…" Laura shakes her head. *Oh, what the hell.*

"Na … nauseated?" he stutters.

"Mm. Car or sea sickness? That sort of a thing?"

"Nnh … no."

Laura nods, then taps four short commands in. "Might want to look away anyway."

Four of the mortals' heads lift up from the floor— her daughter being one of them—until their skulls crash hard against the white tiles. Blood slowly pools around their heads.

"One of your wires is loose," Laura says to the hyperventilating man. None of the wires matter anymore, but she wants to give Baldwin something to do so he won't panic too much and pass out.

She walks around the see-through wall, preparing the remaining three brains. When Baldwin fingers the wires on his helmet and follows one to the power processor, Laura enters the short commands for patients three, six, and seven. She glances at the big man—Yeti—shaking her head slowly. "You're a lucky bastard if you can pull this off."

Three more heads pop up and crash against the floor. The pool of blood grows, now reaching Baldwin's shoes by the processor. When he notices the blood, he turns to look. He dives over the operating table—vomiting.

"I told you not to look."

"Are they . . . are they dead?"

Laura ignores his question. "You want some nitrous, Robert?"

He screams in panic, stepping away from the pool of blood and toward the spiral staircase.

"You can't go upstairs, Robert. The wires aren't long enough, and the smoke will only kill you faster."

Without answering, he cries and stumbles on his own feet. Just before falling, Baldwin grabs onto the staircase's railing and ends up sitting down on the lowest stair. "They . . . they're all dead, Laura. I don't . . . I don't want to die."

A happy squealing sound echoes from the white glow, in the direction of Luna's room. One, two, four, and five must have arrived.

"They're not dead, Robert. Don't be silly."

Luna's happy screaming gets louder. Laura's hand twitches toward the mute button, but then returns to the keyboard. She picks off an invisible piece of lint from her sleeve, fighting not to smile.

A loud crash echoes through the mansion. The east side wall has collapsed, the flames pushing in fast. Thick smoke travels in, making it hard to see Baldwin, huddled by the stairs.

Laura circles the wall, counting seven green checkmarks on her newly created databases. A short-lived grin stretches her face, then she clears her throat and returns her focus to the blubbering man gripping the stairway railing, screaming at the top of his lungs.

"Okay, Robert. You have to detach your emotions from . . . " When his screaming gets louder, Laura shakes her head and enters the last command code into the eighth folder on the wall. What's the use of trying to calm down a man who thinks he's about to die?

Tap.

The screaming ends. The smoke engulfs the mansion's hallway, blocking all camera views. Laura swipes her hand lazily to the left, killing the camera feed.

A man's flickering image appears by the edge of the egg's glowing white balcony: Baldwin, wearing his stained white lab coat. He blinks rapidly, still holding onto an imaginary stairway railing.

Laura doesn't move closer to him. Nor does she rush to the egg either, to comfort and welcome her uploaded daughter. But for a fleeting moment, she feels more alive than ever before. She keeps stroking the rabbit's soft hair.

She's not human anymore. She's not a computer, program, or an algorithm either. She's more than that. A savior. The chosen one. Unstoppable.

She's the revenant.

EPILOGUE
KRISTIAN

"What is this shit?" As though he's walking through a foggy field, he tries to clear his head enough to make sense of his surroundings. A strange vibration tickles his face as he follows Luna through the strangest place he's ever seen in his life. The forest looks familiar, and at the same time, completely . . . *wrong*.

"Luna, what is this goddamn place?"

The Serbian woman—or at least what's left of her earthly form—jumps happily in front of him. She turns, clapping her hands together in excitement. "You like it? Just wait until you see the cabin."

Kristian stops on the slightly vibrating forest floor. "A cabin?"

Luna turns around but keeps walking backward. "Don't mock it till you see it. It's really fucking cool."

"Bill and Micky get a castle by the ocean, and I get a moldy cabin in the middle of the woods?"

"Why do you have to be such a grump all the time?" Luna scolds him, but her smile never ceases.

"You're the fucking grump . . ." Kristian mumbles but follows Luna deeper into the cyber forest. He looks around the space, a million questions circling his mind, but he has no actual words to ask them out loud.

It could have been a minute, could have been only a few seconds, but suddenly a log cabin rises in front of them. Time acts differently around here. Like it doesn't really exist. It's one of the things he wants to ask Luna about, but he doesn't have the words to do so.

Luna stops by a majestic log cabin. "Here we are."

"Huh . . ."

"What's that, grump?"

Kristian steps up on the porch and runs his hand on the railing's fine wood. "It's not half bad."

"Told you."

Luna marches past him and opens the heavy door into the cabin. Without following her in, Kristian asks, "Did you create this place? Or did Solomon?"

"All me, my friend," her chirpy voice calls from inside the cabin. "Why?"

"Just wondering."

"You got a problem with Laura?"

Baffled, Kristian steps inside the cabin and stares at Luna. "You *don't* have a problem with Laura?"

A brief laugh is all the answer he gets. And then his mind wanders off toward a whole new mystery. He scans the inside of the cabin with his gaze.

A dozen dumbbells.

Shelves, stocked with protein bars and power shakes.

Posters of half-naked women carrying rifles.

"What is this shit?" he asks for what seems like the hundredth time.

"It's me. Guessing." Luna shrugs happily. "Did I get any of it right? Do you want anything else? Just tell me, and I'll make it happen."

So she created this place. The cabin. The furniture. Code snippets—that's all this is. The thought of objects disappearing or appearing from the vibrating air is too much for him to bear. Kristian waves his hand. "Don't bother."

"No really. You can have anything you want here. *All* you want, actually."

All I want is her, Kristian thinks. He swallows in a way that should hurt his throat. But just like time, pain doesn't seem to exist here either.

"How about a minibar?"

He waves Luna off again, suddenly feeling drained and dislocated beyond anything he's ever felt. Can he sleep it off? Will he ever sleep again?

"A pool, then. With a Hawaiian-style bar."

"Luna, you're really starting to piss me off."

"Because I want you to have nice things? To make you feel at home?"

He blows a raspberry. "This place might be many things, Luna. But *home* is definitely not one of them."

"Okay." Luna crosses her arms, tapping her index finger on her lower lip. After a moment of blissful silence, she chirps out again. "The season. That's what's wrong. It needs to be dark and snowy."

Just as Luna is about to leave the cabin, Kristian grabs her arm and gently pulls her to a stop. "Listen, ding-dong. Just because I'm from Finland doesn't mean that I like polar nights and snowmen. Just chill. Okay?"

After a deep, dramatic sigh, Luna leans against the cabin's doorway. Pouting, she stares him down. "Name one thing."

"What?"

"Let me give you one thing you really want, and I'll leave you be."

His sigh matches Luna's. "Fine." He spreads his arms, gesturing a truce. "Give me wood."

Her eyes widen. "Listen, buddy. I know I said I'd give you anything—"

"A *woodshed*." He rolls his eyes at her. "And some tools."

Her whole face brightens. Standing straight, Luna swipes the air and starts fiercely tapping onto a floating keyboard. Kristian turns his gaze, the odd view too overwhelming for him to witness.

Is this how it feels to be dead?

"Like that?" Luna asks, stepping outside onto the porch. Kristian follows her.

A low-roofed shed with a tall stack of firewood rises just outside the cabin. The blue-tinted grass is now covered with a thin layer of snow. Kristian extends his hand. Snowflakes land on his palm, but he can't feel their cold bite.

"Is it big enough?" Luna asks.

"Size doesn't really matter."

"That's what she said." Luna grins at him. "But we all know that's not true."

Grunting, Kristian turns and walks back into the cabin. At the corner of the spacious room, a queen size bed with inviting bedding stands in the corner. He sits down on the bed, running his hand on the smooth sheets.

"You can actually taste the protein bars," Luna says. "And there's fresh fruit in the kitchen too." Luna walks around, an excited bounce in her step. "I wasn't sure what kind of books you liked, so I went with murder mysteries. You read, right?"

"Yeah, I read. But I'm more of a pistachio and Donald Duck kind of a guy."

After a few seconds of blinking, Luna raises her hand to pull out her magical computer.

"No, hey. Stop. Enough of that for now." He gives her a quick smile, hoping it'll make up for his grouchy tone of voice. "No more magic tricks. Please."

"What's wrong?"

"I'm just tired, is all."

"I get that," Luna says, crossing her hands behind her back. "Sorry. I know it's a lot." When Kristian doesn't respond, Luna turns to leave the cabin. She points at something outside by the woodshed. "Just don't let Owena play with that axe when she visits." Luna waves her hand, about to leave.

"Hold on."

Her friendly face peeks back in, eyebrows raised.

"What do you mean, when Owena visits?"

"Man, I know you're a loner. But trust me, this place will drive you nuts way faster if you don't hang out with the rest of us. Take it from someone who's been stuck here with Dr. Buzzkill for what seems like a decade."

"I get that. And I agree." Frowning, Kristian reaches for a protein bar and tosses it up in the air, catching it again. "Can I visit anyone I want?"

"In the egg?" Luna waves for him to follow her outside. She walks to the woodshed and gestures around them. "See that purple glow?"

At first, all Kristian sees is the endless cyber forest and snow. Then, a tiny purple light catches his eye in the distance. "Yeah."

"That's my room. You can come knocking whenever you'd like."

"Okay . . ." Slowly, he spins around on the spot, scanning the blue-tinted forest. After a moment of searching, a red glow appears between the birch trees in the distance. He points at the light. "Who's that?"

"Owena and Sanna. And right next to them is the main entrance to the egg and the balcony . . ."

"You mean Solomon?"

Luna nods.

"Yeah, pass." Lowering his gaze, Kristian shifts his weight from one foot to another. He glances at Luna, then looks over her shoulder. "And Kaarina's door?"

It's Luna's turn to twist her hands and avoid Kristian's gaze. After a nervous smile, she points into the distance at a bright green light. "But I haven't finished showing you around. That's the castle, but Bill is much more private than Micky, so I wouldn't just barge in. Not to mention Maria . . ."

"Luna."

She inhales sharply, then sighs and shakes her head. "She doesn't want to see you."

Her words make Kristian jerk his head back. *No. Not this. Anything but this.*

"Listen, man. It's probably just the shock of all this. Uploads are not exactly on the low end of the cultural shock scale. Give her some time."

"It's not because of the upload." Kristian grabs the axe and places a log on a wide stump by the cabin. He swings and the wood splits in half, landing softly on the snowy ground.

"It's not?"

"No."

It's because she lost Markus, he thinks, but can't bear to say it out loud.

Another log splits in half under his axe.

"Listen, Yeti . . . "

"Don't call me that." Again, the axe lands on the stump, sending more firewood flying through the air. "You've seen my file. You know my real name."

"I don't . . . I didn't look."

Kristian's axe stops midair. He turns his head to investigate Luna's face. "Quit your bullshit, Luna. The laughing gas, the upload . . . You needed my chip number for it all."

"And that's all I did. Looked up the number."

A grunt. He lets the axe fall hard on the stump. "It's Kristian."

She crosses her arms and grins happily. "No shit."

"No shit, what?"

"Nothing. Just not what I expected."

"What did you expect?"

Luna chuckles briefly. "I don't know. I still think Yeti fits better than Kristian."

Kristian rolls his eyes. Then he leans on the axe, staring past Luna. To his surprise, Luna lets him gather his thoughts in peace. She doesn't tap her foot or fidget nervously because of the silence. She just watches the non-cold snowflakes fall, momentarily mesmerized by the sight. Kristian wants to ask her why she's decided to make the snow warm instead of cold, but the question washes away as his mind fills with ten new ones.

"What's the purpose?" he asks Luna instead. "Us, being here."

A familiar grin visits Luna's face. "The meaning of life? Man, I've had some tough questions from everyone so far, but that's quite the opener."

"You know what I mean."

A shrug. "Anything you want."

He grabs the axe and swings it over his shoulder. "I want to fix it."

"Fix what?"

"What's happening . . . " Kristian gestures at the ground he stands on. "Down there. The real world. Home."

Her nods are careful, yet Luna fails to hide her excitement. "Okay." She gives him a smile. "Jovan and

I could definitely use an extra pair of hands to take down Nurse Saarinen."

"But that's the thing," Kristian says. "How do we do that from here?"

"Same way we did before. We outsmart her."

"But we have no . . ." Kristian hesitates, the thoughts rushing through his muddled mind.

"Have no what?"

"Hands. Arms. Legs."

"Since when have we needed limbs to manipulate the human mind?"

He exhales and shakes his head. "Cut the bullshit, Luna. Just lay it on me."

"Social media. The AR. All the Happiness crap. None of that was ever forced on people. They opted for it themselves."

He pauses to think. "True."

Luna smacks her hands together. The sound is off, like she's wearing thick mittens though Kristian can't see any. "It's settled then. You'll start working with us whenever you're all settled in and ready."

"No."

"No?"

"I want to start now."

Luna blinks at him, scoffing but smiling. "But you just got up here."

Kristian lets the axe drop on the stump. "I did." He wipes his hands together, knowing very well they will never again have wood dust, stains, or calluses on them. "And now I want to kick some rogue nurse ass. Where do we begin?"

THE END

Shoot! Book 10 of the Unchipped story is at a close. But don't worry, you can find out what happens next in Book 11 in the Unchipped series, DECHIPPED: KRISTIAN!

My dearest reader,

You are simply amazing! Thank you so much for your support and readership! I can't tell you how much you reading this book means to me. I'm humbled and honored that you've dedicated your valuable time to experience the Unchipped universe with me. I'm still a newbie author, so if you were to leave me a review on the store you purchased this from, or Goodreads it would be a huge help! Short or long, doesn't matter. Reviews are the best way to help other readers find the Unchipped Series.

Want to stay in touch? I would love it if you'd subscribe to my newsletter:

@ www.TayaDeVere.com/HappinessProgram

You can also find me on:

Facebook........................@TayaDeVereAuthor

Instagram.......................@TayaDeVere_Author

Goodreads......................@TayaDeVere

Bookbub........................@Taya-DeVere

Gratefully yours,
Taya

About the Author

Taya DeVere is a Finnish science fiction writer who loves telling stories about perfectly imperfect people in dystopian and postapocalyptic settings. Her characters are outsiders and rebels who stand up against injustice and form unlikely friendships with other rebels along the way. She is the writer of more than 21 books, and is always developing new stories to delight her readers. Taya's restless feet have taken her all over Finland, the United Kingdom, Spain, and North America. She lived in the United States for seven years but is currently based in Turku, Finland with her partner, Chris.

Best things in life: friends & family, memories made, and mistakes to learn from. Taya also loves licorice ice cream, secondhand clothes and things, bunny sneezes, salmiakki, and sauna.

Dislikes: clowns, the Muppets, Moomin trolls, dolls (especially porcelain dolls), human size mascots, and celery.

Taya's writing is inspired by the works of authors like Margaret Atwood, Peter Heller, Hugh Howey, and Blake Crouch.

Final Thanks

This book was so much fun to write! And then… it was time to edit it. Tying together multiple storylines and points of view's is challenging for me, to say the least. The further the story goes, the more my mind muddles and jumps around the timeline. Lucky me, I have two of the most outstanding editors and two equally brilliant proofreaders to help me with the "unmuddling" – also known as the editing process. The best part is, my team is equally excited about the characters and the Unchipped story as it develops and molds into this epic, futuristic adventure.

A thousand times THANK YOU, Lindsay, Chris Thompson, Laura Lennig, and Chris DeVere, for all the hours you spend brainstorming and problem solving this story. I adore and appreciate each and every one of you.

www.ingramcontent.com/pod-product-compliance
Lightning Source LLC
Chambersburg PA
CBHW010428120726
47992CB00010B/3359